A TRAP IS SPRUNG

The Planet X ship that had crashed on the tiny Neptunian moon, showed up clearly against the barren landscape. Simon landed the *Icarius* next to it, and then he and Bob and Juan advanced toward it.

A find like this could change the course of the war. With alien weapons to study, Federation scientists could alter the balance of power and perhaps even avert the ultimate clash and catastrophe.

But something was wrong . . . and very strange.

Bob stopped to look. The hull of the ship hadn't been driven into the ground. It was cut off sharply just below the center, as if someone had taken a giant cleaver and sliced down one side.

Amazing! This was no ship, but a mere mock-up. Just fabric stretched over a metal frame.

Bait for a trap . . . and they were in it!

The Mysterious Planet

Lester del Rey

A Del Rey Book

BALLANTINE BOOKS ● **NEW YORK**

A Del Rey Book
Published by Ballantine Books

Library of Congress Catalog Card Number: 52-14254

ISBN 0-345-30418-7

This edition published by arrangement with Holt, Rinehart and
Winston

Manufactured in the United States of America

First Ballantine Books Edition: April 1978
Third Printing: June 1982

Cover art by David B. Mattingly

To
Scott and Sidney Meredith

CONTENTS

CHAPTER 1 /

A Brand New World

IT WAS A FINE MORNING on Mars, clear, crisp and cold. In a little over a hundred years the great air factories had increased the oxygen content until it could be breathed without a mask, and had added enough carbon-dioxide gas to let the air collect and hold the faint heat of the sun. Now it was like a morning high in the mountains on Earth.

Bob Griffith breathed in deeply, enjoying the piney scent of Martian cactus, and let his breath out again in a frosty whirl. After nine months at the Space Academy on Earth, it was good to be home again. He stopped at the entrance to the Space Navy port to glance back at the city of Tharsis, where the Naval Administration building rose up with elfin grace possible only on a world of light gravity. That and the port had dominated his dreams since he was old enough to know that he wanted to be a naval officer, like his father.

Still a few weeks short of seventeen, Bob was already beginning to look like a man. He was still growing, lacking two inches of six feet, and his body hadn't fully rounded out; but the fur parka he wore now concealed his slimness. The quiet seriousness of his face seemed to add a couple of years to his age, though his gray eyes held hints of fire in them. Normally, a cowlick in his brown hair would have added a touch of humor, but the typical crew-cut of an Academy cadet had removed that, much to Bob's satisfaction.

1

He started through the port entrance now, being careful of his stride. This was his first morning back from Earth, and the light gravity of Mars seemed almost strange to him, though he'd grown up there. Then the sight of the great port with its hangars and ships pointing to the stars hit him, and he forgot everything else—even the question he'd been hoping his father would answer, once the normal morning duties of a Wing Commander were over.

Bob walked down the line of ships. Cruisers like slim, needle-nosed cigars; little pursuit jobs; big battlewagons, massive with armor and bristling with guns . . .

He came to a sudden halt, blinking his eyes. In a corner of the field, a sleek little private ship stood proudly, glistening with newness, and completely out of place on a military field. Bob looked for a sign of naval insignia and found none. There was only the name painted on the tail—the *Icarius*.

"Hi, Bob." The voice came from near the little ship, and Bob dropped his eyes to see Simon Jakes slouching out from behind a fin. "Thought it was you. How d'you like the bus? Dad gave it to me for my eighteenth birthday . . . sort of made up for the Academy's kicking me out!"

Bob muttered under his breath, but he moved toward the other. Jakes was probably the richest boy in the Solar Federation, since his father owned Federal Space Shipping. But the boy looked like early caricatures of a dumb country hick—the kind probably never seen outside the movies. Coarse yellowish hair fell forward over his forehead, and his eyes seemed vacant in his flat face. His thick lips were always parted slightly, from an early case of adenoids, and a prominent Adam's apple bobbed on his throat while he talked. His body was a good six feet tall, but his slump and drooping shoulders made him seem shorter.

Yet he was intelligent enough, Bob knew. Nobody had liked him at Space Academy, where he'd been in Bob's platoon; but it probably wasn't all Jakes's fault.

Too much money, his appearance, and a delayed education by tutors had all been against his chances of winning friends. Then, when he couldn't take discipline and his father had tried to keep him in the Academy by pulling political strings, it had increased the dislike of the other cadets. Bob felt almost sorry for Jakes, but couldn't entirely like him, either.

Now Simon Jakes came over, trying to be too friendly, as always. "Come on in, Bob, and look her over. Hey, you look good! Don't mind me—just got up. Flew in last night, just getting breakfast."

"How come you're on naval grounds?" Bob wanted to know. He hesitated, looking at the little ship. He really should go on to see his father, but this was the first time he'd really looked at one of the super-deluxe private yachts.

Simon, obviously bursting with pride, was beaming as Bob followed him slowly into the ship. "*Icarius* has the new hydrogen drive, and the regular yards can't service her. So Dad got a special permit for me to use the Navy shops. Isn't she a beaut?"

Bob had to admit it. Simon didn't keep it polished up, as a Navy man would have done, but the gleaming interior was the last word in luxury. There was even real cream for the cocoa Simon poured out.

"Took just four days here from Earth," Simon went on. "Like a dream. You come on the *Mars Maid*? Yeah, I thought so. Boy, I wouldn't travel on a liner after riding this! The minute Dad got my unlimited pilot's license fixed—took plenty of greasing to get it, too —the very minute, off I took. And here I am!"

"Yeah, here you are," Bob agreed, without enthusiasm. He wondered if Jakes had any idea of how sickening the idea of bribing officials for an unlimited license was. The mechanical beauty of the inside of the *Icarius* suddenly lost its interest for him. "Well, I have to be going, Simon. See you around, I guess."

Simon's face fell, making him look more like a clown than ever. "Oh!" Then he shook his head. "Nope, you won't see me much, Bob. I'm heading out pretty soon."

"Pirates are supposed to be operating beyond the asteroids," Bob told him. "They'd pick you up in a hurry and hold you for ransom. At least there are rumors that pirates are operating again. The *Ganymede Gal* was found stripped with nobody on board. That's why the Outfleet is getting ready here."

The Navy was no longer maintained to fight wars. Once, a hundred years before, there had been a close call, when Mars, Venus, and Earth all began building up their private navies and starting a quarrel over rights to the moons of Jupiter. But men of good sense and good will had stopped it in time; the fleets had been united into one Space Navy under the Solar Federation. They had been used to prevent piracy, make sure there could never be another threat of space war, and do the general work of a sort of space coast guard. For years, piracy had been stamped out, but now rumors were flying thick that it was coming back.

Jakes grinned. "No pirate could catch the *Icarius*, Bob. This ship has legs under her! She'll beat your best Navy cruiser! Anyhow, I hear rumors that the Outfleet's preparing for other things. You heard about Planet X?"

Bob nodded. He'd been on his way to ask his father about that very subject. He'd caught a little of it on the radio while on the way to Mars, and everyone here was talking about it. But there seemed to be very little information. Apparently a world had been found coming in from beyond Pluto—the tenth planet that had been speculated on by astronomers since 1900.

The reporters had named it Planet X, because X stood for ten and also for unknown.

"What about it, anyhow?" he asked.

Jakes grinned, and opened a panel on the control board of the *Icarius*. "Ultrafrequency radio-printer," he boasted. "Only one ever installed on a private ship. Get all the dope right from Earth as fast as Dad's private connections get ahold of it. Neat, eh? And look what came over it."

He passed a few sheets of paper across, and Bob studied them. They gave what he already knew, with a lot more. Planet X was estimated at about the size of Earth, and of equal density. Then he gasped. Planet X wasn't outside the orbit of Pluto—it was between Pluto and Neptune. Its orbit was now known not to be circular, but egg-shaped, with the small end of the oval reaching a distance of less than three billion miles from the sun, and the large end estimated as reaching out to about seven billion miles, far beyond Pluto. It looked like a crazy orbit, but that was only part of it.

In one month, since first spotted, it had covered nearly fifty million miles. At such a distance from the sun, it should have been crawling along slowly—yet it was traveling at twice the speed of Earth in defiance of all laws of planetary orbits!

Then he saw the message was copied from one of the more sensational Earth papers, and stopped wondering about it. The reporter was going into great detail about its being a "mystery planet" because of its speed, but that paper was never accurate. They'd probably just put the decimal point in the wrong place.

"So your father's keeping tabs on you?" Bob asked, as he handed back the sheets with a poker face. It was a dirty crack, but he couldn't resist it.

Jakes flushed deeply and frowned. "No such thing. He's too busy for that. I'm paying his private secretary plenty to send me all the news on X."

"For what? The Navy can get information direct, without your help."

"Cut it out, Bob." Jakes frowned again, and then shrugged. "You should guess why I want the information. I'm going to investigate that planet in the *Icarius*—maybe be the first man to land on it. This little ship's as fast as any Navy ship, and she's fueled to go there and back ten times."

Bob grabbed for the sheets again, and checked. He

was right—Space Navy was in charge of investigations, and had marked Planet X as unsafe for civilians until it could be tested officially. He pointed it out silently to Jakes.

The other grinned. "Sure. They want all the glory—that's why they're going to move the Outfleet to Neptune to study X. But until I land there, they can't stop me—and after I do, nobody's going to stop me! I'll be a hero!"

"You'll be a fool!" Bob told him hotly. "That's why you got kicked out of Space Academy—for doing just such fool things against orders. I should report you to the Fleet Commander."

"Won't do any good," Jakes said. "You can't prove it, and my father can get me clearance out of the port, as long as I say I'm just going to Neptune—nothing illegal about that."

He could probably get away with it, since citizens were expected to co-operate voluntarily with the Navy, and usually did so. But it left a bad taste in Bob's mouth. He got up and started out again; some of his feeling must have shown, since Jakes suddenly made an effort to laugh.

"Aw, I'm just needling you, Bob," he said quickly. "I'm going to Neptune, sure—I've got clearance for that. I probably won't try to reach Planet X first. I could, though. The *Icarius* could beat anybody."

"Maybe. But she isn't carrying six-inch armor, like a battlewagon. Anyhow, I've got to be going. Better keep your pretty little toy away from the Outplanets, Si."

Jakes saw him to the port, grinning more easily. "Jealous, eh?" he fired as his parting shot.

Bob shrugged and went down the pedestrian walk toward headquarters. Jakes's crack rankled a bit, because he knew he *was* jealous. He had no real desire for a private yacht, but he couldn't help resenting the fact that Jakes would be able to be on the front line if anything proved interesting about Planet X. Part of his resentment probably came from the fact that his father hadn't even told him the Outfleet was heading for Neptune.

Then he grinned ruefully at his thoughts. He had been back only one night, and the usual family reunion had taken up all the time. He had no right letting Simon Jakes get under his skin. After all, he'd been on his way to ask his father about Planet X, and he could still do it.

Bob's father was just leaving his office at the end of Wing Nine's hangar when Bob got there. The older man was a perfect picture of what a Wing Commander should be—erect, well-muscled without fat, with a face that held command and self-confidence without being either stern or proud. His uniform was strictly regulation, without the fancy cut that some men affected. The deep gray trousers and jacket were without ornamentation, except for the golden sun on his collar.

His voice was warm and relaxed. "Morning, Bob. Thought you might be around, so I've been killing time. Want to come along while I check our loading schedule?"

He took the answer for granted and headed for the front of the hangar. Then he suddenly stopped, and swung about with a grin on his face.

"You might as well know it now, Bob," he said. "You're looking at the man who's been selected to investigate Planet X! My orders were just confirmed this morning."

Bob blinked, and nearly stumbled. "You *have!*" he gasped, and then felt foolish at the treble note that had crept into his voice. "Here I was just coming to ask if you knew anything about it. Why didn't you tell me last night? You must have known."

"Naturally," Commander Griffith agreed. "But not officially. And we don't spread rumor in the Navy, boy. I was just going to tell the men about it."

He turned again and Bob followed him. He was all confused now. He was glad his father had the assignment; he knew it would be a prize chance for advancement toward the coveted position of Fleet Commander; every man in the Fleet had probably wanted the opportunity, and his father had gotten it! But again a twinge of jealousy hit at him.

If he'd been two years older, and commissioned, he could have been going, maybe. But now he'd have to stay here on Mars, without even the companionship of his father, until the Academy opened again.

It was probably the last chance for exploration he would ever know. The planets had all been covered, years before; and the stars were still out of reach, and wouldn't be touched during his lifetime. Now a brand new planet showed up—and the best he could do would be to read about it!

Obviously, official word had already been beaten by the rumors, since the men of Wing Nine were clumped into little groups around their twenty ships when Bob and Commander Griffith reached them. They broke up at once, grinning, and began descending on the two.

Griffith halted them with a wave of his hand. "It's official, boys. We're heading out for Outpost by Neptune in three days. We base there, scout Planet X, and land to explore if it looks feasible. If not, we're to determine the orbit of the planet exactly. And it's no secret now that Planet X is heading inward at a speed that makes some of the astronomers think it must be from outer space, and not a real planet at all! So it should be interesting!"

A whoop went up from them, and the younger men began a crazy snake dance in and out among the ships.

Griffith grinned broadly, and turned back to Bob. "There's one little thing I forgot to tell you," he said, too casually. He stopped to light his pipe, then met Bob's eyes suddenly. "I got special permission to take along a junior aide—some young fellow from the Academy, for instance. Any suggestions?"

Bob's mouth really fell open then. He stared up at his

father, not quite daring to believe what the other was saying. "You mean . . ."

Griffith nodded. "I mean you, of course! You know the old tradition—on anything except the most dangerous special mission, the Academy usually places one of its cadets as a reward for good work. It keeps up interest. This time you were on the list of students recommended, and Fleet Commander Jonas thought it might be a good idea for me to have my own son along."

Bob stood still, unable to make a sound more meaningful than a yell. Then he let out another shout, and leaped forward into the snake dance, adding his cries to those of the other men.

And he'd been jealous of Jakes! This was better than anything that Jakes could hope for. It was even better than graduating from the Academy with top honors and getting command of a ship at once. It was like . . .

He gave up trying to think what it was like, and just went along with the rest of the shouting, happy group from Wing Nine.

CHAPTER 2 /

Attack in Space

JAKES CAME TO SEE BOB the night before the take-off. Bob's mother announced it when Bob came in from his final fitting for his uniform, which would bear the insignia of a Cadet Observer—a triangle with a dot inside. Her still pretty face was a mixture of worry over last-minute details and maternal pride, and she nearly forgot it.

Then she caught herself. "You've got a visitor, Bobby. I took him up to your room. Simon Jakes. Wasn't he in the Academy with you?"

Bob grimaced slightly, and nodded. "What did he want?"

"I don't know—he didn't say. I gave him some cookies and soda, and left him looking at your model collection. He seemed like a nice boy."

All Bob's friends seemed like nice boys, to her. And all who had ever come had been stuffed with cookies and soda. Sometimes Bob wondered whether she realized that he and the boys he knew were no longer ten years young. Then he remembered that she'd taken the news of his coming trip without a moment's protest, like a good Navy woman, and he felt ashamed of himself. He caught her around the shoulders in a quick hug, and went up to his room.

Jakes surprised him. He looked up and saw Bob, and jumped to his feet with one hand stretched out. "Hey, Bob, you lucky dog! Congratulations. I just heard.

11

Might have told a fellow. Couldn't be happier if it happened to me."

"I meant to see you . . ." Bob began, but the other nodded.

"Sure, I guess you've been busy. So've I. Been trying to get them to move up my take-off schedule, but your flight has all the priorities."

"Then you're still planning on being the foolhardy hero?" Bob asked.

"I dunno. Maybe not. From what I hear, I figure I'd better take it easy. I've got clearance to Neptune and official permission to base the *Icarius* at Outpost Field; with all this stir over Wing Nine, that took some doing, too. But now I'm trying to get a chance to join your party."

He stopped, and Bob shook his head. "Go along officially? How?"

"Oh, it's been done," the other answered. "Dad heads the pool of commercial interests that would have to help develop Planet X if it has ores and such things. Sometimes the Fleet takes along a commercial observer or two. I thought maybe you could put in a good word with your father, and that might help."

So that was the angle? Bob shook his head quickly. "It wouldn't help. Dad makes his own decisions, and he's already decided there'd be no more in the party."

"Oh! Well, no harm trying." Jakes seemed to drop it completely, to Bob's surprise. "Anyhow, I'm going to keep working on it. If I can't go officially . . . well, somehow I'm going to get a look at Planet X, but we'll see. Can I give you a hand with anything?"

Bob shook his head, just as his mother came to announce that dinner was on the table, and that a place had already been set for Jakes. Simon seemed almost embarrassed at being included, but he was quick to accept; apparently he wasn't used to being included in groups. Then the talk broke down into generalities until Jakes left, and Bob and his father could begin discussing the details of the official trip.

The ships were all fueled and provisioned to the last bit, though much of that seemed useless, since Outpost was well equipped to supply them. Partly, it was just routine Navy precaution, but there seemed to be an added element of caution involved. Griffith admitted that he didn't know what was behind it, unless it had something to do with the increase of piracy beyond the orbit of Jupiter.

Having secured leave, the men, of course, were out celebrating their last night on Mars. And the ships were already lined up outside the hangar, waiting for take-off. They stood on their tail fins, rising some two hundred feet into the thin air, seeming already straining toward space. Griffith's flagship, the heavy cruiser *Lance of Deimos* headed them, rearing up another fifty feet.

Bob's own preparations were complete. As a Cadet Observer, he was entitled to one bag, weighing not over thirty pounds, and it was already packed. He tried to think of something else to do, and then sat fiddling uncomfortably, until his father suggested a game of darts that took up the rest of the evening.

Weather control had deliberately made sure it was a fine morning for the take-off; there wasn't a cloud in the sky. Bob and his family drove up a few minutes late, since there had been some delay in getting his uniforms. A crowd was already assembled, seeing the men of Wing Nine off.

Bob's mother was an old hand at this. She didn't get out of the car or carry on as some of the other women were doing. She kissed her husband quickly, squeezed Bob's hand, and managed a perfectly normal smile at them. "Good luck, sailors," she told them, and then began backing the car out of the way, where she could watch the take-off. Bob found himself swallowing quickly, but he tried to keep a stiff, military pose.

He waited in line to be checked in, while his father went on ahead. He was beginning to think the line would never move up when Simon Jakes jumped out of a taxi and came rushing up, obviously looking for him. Jakes was sweating, but he broke into his usual slack-lipped grin as he spotted Bob.

"Whew! Thought I'd missed you. Here!" He shoved a box into Bob's hands awkwardly. Bob turned it over and finally opened it. Inside was an officer's pocket-knife, a marvel of compactness that held twelve tools, from scissors to tiny pliers, as well as standard blades. Beside it lay one of the tiny, expensive little personal radios issued to the higher officers. It was built to fit entirely within one ear, except for the nearly invisible wire that served as an antenna and connected to the walnut-sized power pack to be worn in the breast pocket. Bob had wanted one for a long time, but the price had always been prohibitive. With it, he would be automatically tuned in to all general calls, and independent of the ship paging system.

He blinked in surprise, instinctively adjusting it to his ear. Then he shook his head. "No can do, Si. Look, it's swell of you, but . . ."

Jakes face sobered quickly. "You mean just because it's expensive? You won't be obligated—Navy pride, all that." He shrugged. "Okay, I was afraid of that. Though why, when you know I'm filthy with the stuff . . ."

"No, I didn't mean that," Bob told him quickly. It had been on his mind, but Jakes's obvious hurt made the excuse impossible; anyhow, the expense hadn't meant much, and the spirit of the gift seemed genuine. "I mean, I'm already right up to the limit on weight."

The smile came back. "Oh that!" Jakes dragged out another parcel quickly. "Yeah, I thought of that. Here. I had the whole thing checked for weight, and this saves enough over your regulation set to make it come out even."

He opened it to show a set of de luxe toilet fittings inside a special case. It was another of the expensive things which was nonregulation, but officially approved for those who wanted to buy them out of their own funds.

Bob gave up, and hastily opened his bag to exchange the toilet set for the heavier regulation one he had packed. He tried to thank Jakes, but the other would have none of it, seeming genuinely happy that his gift had been accepted. Then the checker tapped Bob on the shoulder, and Simon Jakes stuck out his hand.

"See you on Outpost," he said quickly, and was gone.

The checker ran his eyes up Bob's uniform to see if everything had been removed from his pockets for the weighing, and then stamped his permit. He stepped up the little ramp and into the *Lance of Deimos*, an accredited member of the crew.

"Take-off in seven minutes," the little radio said into his ear. "Officers will report to the control room."

Bob stowed his luggage in the tiny bunk room he would occupy, and made for the control room on the double. Technically, while he had few duties beyond serving as a runner for his father, he was one of the officers and subject to all such general calls. Engineers, and other officers concerned with the mechanical end of the ship, were listed as reporting when they were at their own stations, and had their intercommunication phones switched on. Actually, only the dour Dutch navigator, Hoeck, and the Senior Leftenant, Anderson, would be there, together with his father. Griffith believed in operating with the minimum number of officers permitted.

The others were already in their seats when Bob came in. His father blinked in surprise at the sight of the radio in Bob's ear, but he gave no other notice. Bob dropped into the seat that would normally have been occupied by a Junior Leftenant. Then the radio began buzzing with Griffith's voice as the time ran out and the ships reported in. Outside the field was cleared and the green flag was going up.

Commander Griffith put down the little microphone and reached for the instrument board. The *Lance of Deimos* let out a thundering growl, and Bob was forced down in the chair as acceleration hit. It was old stuff to him, after the training at the Academy—and yet, it was completely new. He had never been on a real ship, on a genuine mission of importance, before. This gave a flavor to the mission that set his heart pounding heavily, while the *Lance* picked up speed and grew quiet as they left the thin atmosphere behind.

The acceleration picked up then. This was no passenger liner, filled with worldlubbers, but a Navy ship with a trained crew. Every man on board could stand an acceleration pressure that was equal to three times their Earth weight for days. Nobody ever learned to like feeling such "weight," as they did the feeling of weightlessness during times when the ship was just coasting; but the human body was seemingly capable of adapting to almost anything.

Griffith and Hoeck compared notes, and the Commander set the controls. Then he swung his chair around, leaving the ship on its automatic pilot. He faced the others, holding a spacegram in his hand.

"We've had a flash on Planet X," he announced. "It's not for general release yet, without more checking. But it may interest you to know that the Pluto observatory caught something that might have been a radio signal from Planet X. Pluto's a long way off on her orbit, and no other planet got it. But now Outpost claims that they have spotted flashes of light. We'll have to be prepared to face the possibility that there is intelligent life on X!"

Bob caught his breath. It couldn't be human life— and men had never found any other forms of intelligent life on the planets. This might be the most important mission in all history . . .

"Bunk, I'd say," Anderson was stating. "That planet's frozen colder than Pluto—where it's been it would get no heat at all from the sun."

Hoeck shrugged. "Pirates!"

"Maybe," Griffith admitted. "The pirate idea may be possible, though it's a little farfetched. But I have to agree with you, Anderson—no alien life could exist in that frozen a climate. Anyhow, we're not being told there is life—just to be prepared for such an eventuality." He faced Bob then. "Cadet, tell the Chief Gunner I want to see him."

Bob went out on legs that felt weak in the high pressure of acceleration. He knew his father could have called on the intercom, but it was standard tradition to keep a novice spaceman on the run as much as possible, until he completely hardened. He was glad of the chance to get away, before the excitement in his face could show that he hadn't dismissed the idea of life on Planet X. After all, even if it were only a pirate base, it would still be something to experience!

Bob didn't have much time to think about it, though. The ship drove on at a steady three gravities of acceleration, adding five million miles an hour to its speed every day. They were more than sixty million miles beyond Mars at the end of twenty-four hours, and nearly a quarter of a billion at the end of the second day. Jupiter's orbit was getting close, though the big planet itself was on the other side of the sun.

Usually the ships took it somewhat more leisurely, but this was a special mission.

The first few hours of moving about under the pressure weren't too bad. Actually, while his body now seemed to weigh over four hundred and fifty pounds, it wasn't the same thing as trying to carry an additional three-hundred-pound load. Here, the increase in apparent weight was spread evenly over his whole body, and in complete balance. But it was still bad enough.

Then his legs began to scream with fatigue at each step. When he went down from the control room toward the tail, it was all right, but fighting back up was sheer torture. He gritted his teeth and bore it in silence. Finally, while his father ate his dinner, he sent Bob off to his bunk, to lie down; he fell into a sodden slumber without any dreams.

Getting up after his sleep was worse than anything

else. The first few hours, while his legs seemed to be afire, nearly drove him to the unforgivable sin of asking for a break. Then numbness set in, and it was better. Somehow, he got through the second day, and he knew that the worst was past. It would be easier from now on, since his strength had already been developed, and he only needed to harden into the continuous grind.

He was asleep when they crossed the orbit of Jupiter and went heading out toward the orbit of Saturn, which would lie far off to the side.

They were five hundred million miles out from Mars when the heavy acceleration suddenly ceased, leaving only enough to give them a seeming weight equal to that on Earth. The change caught Bob in mid-stride, and he bounced up a bit before he could catch himself, wondering whether anything had happened to the rocket engines.

Then the tiny radio buzzed. "Take a break, men. We'll loaf along like this for an hour. Get a bite to eat, if you like. We're on automatic, so you can go off duty until next call. Bob, come on up, if you want to."

Bob knew then that it was purely routine. Doctors had found that nervous tension built up under high acceleration, and it had to receive a rest after a certain time. During that period there would be no formality, as indicated by Griffith's use of his son's name instead of his rank.

Hoeck was carving a tiny statue out of some hard wood, and Anderson was playing a mouth organ. But Bob's father sat relaxed and ready to answer the questions about the ship which had come up during the trip. The ever-present tea of the Navy was already poured and waiting. Bob dropped down gratefully, feeling as light as a feather in spite of the twinges in his sore muscles. Right then, a whole hour of relaxation seemed like a lot.

But it was only half an hour later when something buzzed sharply on the control panel. Anderson glanced sharply toward the light that would tell whether Sparks, the radioman, was on duty. Then he picked up a pair of phones, and began juggling meters. Nearly every instrument on board had auxiliary controls here.

His fingers began hitting a tiny typewriter rapidly. Then he stopped in midstroke. "Cut off! Commander, look at this." He began trying to signal, but obviously got no further message.

Bob crowded up to study the sheet on the typewriter, but his father summarized it quickly. "SOS from the *Ionian*. She's near by and being attacked by pirates!"

"Must have punctured the radio shack," Anderson cut in sharply. "She's gone silent now."

"Any acknowledgments?" Griffith asked.

"None," Anderson said. "We're the nearest ship to her. It looks like it's up to us to go to the rescue."

CHAPTER 3 /

The Black Ship

CAN WE MATCH HER SPEED?" Griffith snapped out to Hoeck. The navigator jerked the sheet out of the typewriter and began studying the numbers that had been sent to indicate position and speed. His fingers jumped to a little calculator, and began work at interpreting them. Bob heard his father sounding a general alarm for the men to get back to duty on the double.

In front of the control room, a small hatch suddenly snapped open, and a six-inch rifle slid out rapidly, turret-mounted and fully compensated for recoil. He knew that all over the ship the various weapons would be made ready—cannon, guided-missile launchers, self-steering torpedoes, and a maze of others.

"Make it," Hoeck decided, and threw another sheet to Griffith, who studied it, frowning heavily.

Anderson whistled as he saw the results, but went back to his seat at once, and began pulling out a suit of elastic cords and metal reinforcement. The others were doing the same, and the radio buzzed in Bob's ear as general orders came over it for all men to get into high-acceleration harness.

His own harness was under his seat. He began slipping it on and binding it up as quickly as he could. It helped to ease the strain of high pressure by binding the body in a tight elastic sheath that prevented distortion and helped to maintain even blood circulation.

When it was on, he found a button on the seat, which

snapped it back to form a horizontal couch. Men could stand more strain when they lay completely horizontal to it.

"Ten seconds," the radio said. Bob counted under his breath, but he was too fast. He'd reached thirteen before the pressure suddenly seemed to hit him with a leaden hand. His father had raised the acceleration to better than eight times the normal pressure of gravity, and cut on the side steering rockets, all together. Now they'd be turning and doubling in space in an attempt to reach the *Ionian* with the same speed and course she was following.

Bob had been given high-acceleration drills before, but never for as long a time. His brain seemed to go numb, except for a dull ache. His senses reeled and threatened to black out on him. His eyes would not focus, and he couldn't see the others beside him. Nor could he hear them because of the roaring in his ears.

The little radio cut through his daze, carrying his father's strained words. "Sparks, order the other ships to continue on course; they're too slow for this. All men attention. We're going into an encounter with pirates. The *Lance* has to take care of it alone. Ready all weapons, be prepared for unknown number of pirates."

It seemed to take hours, though the high-acceleration flight probably lasted no more than half an hour. Even that was too long, though. They'd arrive worn and tired from the strain, even if the pirates hadn't already done their job and gone sailing off without a trace.

Once piracy had nearly been stamped out, but now it seemed to be bolder than ever. There were rumors that the entire crew and passenger list of a couple of ships had been carried away.

Numbness of the acceleration pressure kept Bob from feeling the excitement that he should have experienced. He was almost completely unconscious by the time the high drive was cut, and they snapped back to light acceleration. He revived almost at once, though, to stare through the observation window, as his father and Hoeck were doing.

There was no sign of either the *Ionian* or pirates; they must have arrived too late! Then Anderson let out a sharp grunt, and cut on the big electronic telescope screen. In it, a bright silvery spindle showed up, with the standard lines of a freighter-passenger combination from one of Jupiter's moons.

"Fool!" Hoeck said harshly.

"You can't expect a merchant captain to take a fix in space without error," Griffith told him. "We're lucky he wasn't more off. But it doesn't look as if he's lucky. How far?"

"Three minutes. We'll overtake them about as fast this way as we would by stopping to calculate a new high-drive jump," Anderson guessed. But it was Hoeck's nod that decided Griffith; the navigator could work such short courses out in his head with reasonable accuracy. Now he was setting up an automatic sequence on the board which would slow them down when they reached the *Ionian*.

Bob stared at the screen, where the ship was growing in size as they drew nearer. Obviously the ship had been surprisingly close to their course and speed before the attack, or they couldn't have done more than slip by too fast to help the other. At interplanetary speeds, a normal meeting in space lasted only fractions of a second. There wouldn't be even time to fire a shot. It was that which made piracy possible, since a Navy ship could be still matching course while the pirates were already bound for their hide-out.

At first it looked as if that had happened this time. Then Anderson pointed to the radar screen. There were two shapes there, one obviously the *Ionian*, and the other larger. It must have been painted jet black, which would explain why it didn't show in the telescope screen.

Then, as Bob looked closer, he could just make it out. It was invisible unless he knew where to look.

Suddenly space seemed to flare up around it. The *Ionian* had obviously fired a torpedo, and it had caught the pirate dead center. In the glare the ship seemed to be about six hundred feet long, as big as a full-sized battlewagon. But its lines were different. It was large and rounded at both ends, with a narrower middle that made it look something like a streamlined dumbbell. There were no vanes or projections of any kind.

Beside Bob, his father sucked in sharply on his breath, just as another torpedo went off. One should have finished the black ship, but nothing seemed to happen, except that space around the ship turned faintly blue, and then gradually sank to red and disappeared.

"Screens!" Anderson barked.

Commander Griffith nodded slowly. "It can't be; science proved that screens capable of soaking up a blast like that are impossible. But he's got them, anyhow. No wonder the pirates are getting bolder. Hey!"

Two torpedoes had caught the black ship dead center. But again it rode them out easily, with only a somewhat stronger glow around it. Bob had read up on the Navy's attempts to get screens, long ago. But nobody had been able to come up with anything which could turn the energy of a violent explosion aside or slow up a projectile enough to do any good. They had talked about twisting space a bit—whatever that meant—but they hadn't been able to do it.

Now the *Lance* was closer to the scene. The black ship seemed not to notice them. It turned about quickly, with no jetting of rockets, and pointed squarely toward the *Ionian*. Something must have been done, but there was no sign aboard the black ship. Yet the nose of the *Ionian* suddenly turned white hot and melted into a metal vapor that spread out rapidly through space.

This time even Hoeck cried out. "Heat ray!"

It was another thing the Navy scientists had worked on, and given up. As they had explained it, anything hot enough to project through space and burn would be too hot to be contained in any instruments needed to handle it.

Now the black ship darted in against the *Ionian,* completely covering the merchant ship from view. It must have been a boarding and looting operation, though no details could be seen. Griffith leaped to the control panel, and a second later the guns of the *Lance* began pounding explosive projectiles at the black ship. They hit, but there was only a faint glow.

A warning gong sounded, and Bob braced himself as Hoeck began twisting the *Lance* to come up against the pirate. Commander Griffith was calling men on the intercom. Now he looked up at Anderson.

"This is emergency enough," he stated. "We're breaking out our own secret weapon. And let's hope it works . . . Hey!"

Hoeck had cut the deceleration and was accelerating again. In the screen, Bob saw the reason. The black ship had pulled away as calmly as if it had been alone in space and was now heading outward toward Neptune. Again, there was no sign of rocket blast. It simply moved, with no sign of how.

"Hold it, Hoeck!" The Commander reached for the emergency controls, again restoring deceleration. "We've got to worry about the people on the *Ionian* first. We can't leave people dying, however much I'd like to catch that pirate!"

Bob groaned, though he knew his father was right.

Half a minute later they had matched speeds with the crippled ship. Men already had the connecting tube ready to snap from the *Lance* to the open lock of the *Ionian,* and Hoeck gentled the cruiser in against the freighter.

"No air inside," the exploring party reported back in a couple of minutes.

That meant that anyone inside who hadn't been able to get into a space suit almost at once would be dead. It usually took several minutes to don the bulky suits, too—longer than life was possible without air.

Griffith nodded as Bob reached into a locker for one of the emergency suits. "Go along, if you like. But stay behind Anderson."

They went down, once the suits were on. Men were waiting in the lock, equipped with cutting tools to free anyone aboard the *Ionian* who might be trapped, or fastened behind airtight bulkheads. They all swung into line behind Anderson, going down the rubbery tunnel and into the air lock of the *Ionian*. There the inner lock was stuck, open a crack, but not enough for entrance; some of the crew were just cutting it free as they went in.

Nobody was on the other side to greet them, and that was a bad sign. Anyone trapped on the vessel should have been waiting eagerly for the rescue party. They went up the catwalk toward the control room. Everything was in fair order, but nobody was there.

"Nothing, Commander," Anderson was reporting back. "No sign of bodies, either. We're going to spread out and go through the ship."

He detailed men off in pairs, to begin at the ruined nose and work back to the engine room. Bob went with Anderson. There was still no sign of bodies. That was stranger than anything else. They hadn't expected too much chance of finding men alive, but the dead should have been scattered around. They worked their way back slowly, opening every door, but nothing showed up.

Anderson cracked open a big hatch and cast the light on his helmet down it. "Storage cargo—completely empty. Bob, can you make out that label on the floor?"

Bob stared at the torn strip of paper, and strained his eyes. "Looks like *Biotics—With Care*," he finally decided.

"Must be right," Commander Griffith's voice came over the radio. "The *Ionian* came from Io, where they raise most of our drugs; and from her rate, she must have been coming straight across from Jupiter to Neptune—probably bringing valuable drugs to Outpost to take care of the possible dangers from Planet X there. Maybe you can't find anyone yet because there were no passengers."

They went on, finding all the freight holds emptied. Finally they reached the engine-room entrance, and waited for the others to catch up.

"Better pray," Anderson advised. "Men might just manage to get back here and seal up. If that hatch is locked, we may find them. If it isn't, then nobody's on board."

One of the men threw himself against the door, and it opened quietly. There was no blast of air. The engine hold was as empty as the rest of the ship, and there were still no bodies lying about. They hunted through the ship again, without finding anyone.

In the control room, Anderson and Bob went through the ship's papers, but those had also been rifled. There was a passenger list, but there was no way of knowing for what trip it was meant. From it, though, they discovered that the *Ionian* normally shipped between Io and Earth, and carried a crew of seventeen, with as many as thirty-five passengers. Her maximum acceleration was listed as just under two gravities of thrust—but that would be enough to build up her present speed if she had come all the way from Jupiter, around the sun, and back through Jupiter's orbit, heading for Neptune.

Anderson found another book, listing equipment. "They carried sixty suits," he reported. "Enough for all the passengers and crew, with a few spares." His young face was sweating, and the blond hair that showed through his helmet was matted down against his forehead. Even at best, the space suits were uncomfortable for long wearing, though men could live in them for days.

At Griffith's suggestion, they went down to search all the lockers for space suits. When they had finished counting, all sixty were still on board.

"All right," the Commander ordered finally. "Come

on back, and make it fast. We'll abandon the *Ionian* until a tug came out and salvage her."

They went back silently. It was completely impossible for the pirates to have taken all the freight and every man on board the ship off in no more than the single minute they had been locked together. Yet it had happened. Everything was beginning to come out the same—the events were impossible, but the black ship had done them, all the same.

Bob's eyes jumped to the radar screen as soon as he was back in the control room of the *Lance of Deimos* and climbing out of his suit. He sighed with relief. The pip on the screen showed that the pirate ship was still within radar range. "Not that we can do much against them," he muttered glumly to himself.

Griffith looked up from the calculations Hoeck was making. "Don't be too sure of that, son," he said. "We've got a few tricks up our own sleeves. The Navy's been secretly testing a proton cannon for years, and we have one of the first working models. Ever hear of it?"

Bob nodded doubtfully. The Sunday Supplements and science fiction magazines had been speculating on it for years, but it had finally been put down as a failure. The idea was that hydrogen should be broken down to electrons and protons. The electrons were to be sent out in one stream, and the protons in another, so that the ship using the weapon wouldn't become electrically charged, as it would have done if either had been ejected alone. The trouble had been that the guns previously made could just blast through a thin sheet of paper.

"You'll see it in action soon," Griffith promised. "And it works. Just a matter of getting the speed of the protons high enough. This will cut through ten feet of steel in less than a second. It's still under security wraps, so keep mum about it, after we hit Outpost. Ready yet, Hoeck?"

The navigator nodded, and indicated the control setup. Griffith pressed the general alert for acceleration and gave the crew ten seconds to strap down for it, after the automatic second warning went off. Bob had just succeeded in getting into his harness when the ship blasted off again.

Either his first dose of high drive had given him more power to stand it or the rest while exploring the *Ionian* had restored him more than he had thought. This time he took it without blacking out and without completely losing the power to focus his eyes. He set his gaze on the radar screen, and waited.

The outline of the black ship on the screen began to grow. At this rate, they'd be up to it in a matter of minutes. Then Bob was going to find out what a real space battle was like.

CHAPTER 4 /

Distress Signal

THERE WAS NO SIGN that the black ship had seen them, though it must have had radars as sensitive as their own, judging by the other scientific marvels they had witnessed. Bob kept wondering about them. It was as if some great genius had turned to crime and put the pirates ahead of the rest of the system.

But he knew that was ridiculous. A genius would have no need to turn to crime—he could make more by remaining lawful, and with much less risk. The only reason many of the great scientists were not rich was that they preferred pure research to the type of life needed to amass a fortune. And the idea of a scientist mad enough to enjoy crime was silly; anything so warping to his thoughts would make him anything but a level-headed scientist.

Besides, great inventions were seldom the result of one man's work. It took a genius, plus teams of trained men, plus an amazing amount of equipment.

Maybe the miracles weren't miracles, he suddenly thought. If the *Ionian* had been captured before . . . then the "torpedoes" could have been harmless magnesium-oxygen flares. The melting nose of the ship could have been thermite placed inside and set off by radio, and the almost instantaneous removal of crew and freight would have been a pure fake.

He tried to call out the idea. Then his eyes located the telescope screen, and he relaxed. It didn't account for all the facts. The ship was still blasting along, without any normal trail of rocket exhaust. That couldn't be faked! Anyhow, what good would it be to attempt to trap the *Lance of Deimos,* unless the pirate ship really did have superior weapons?

He gave up the idea reluctantly, but it simply didn't explain enough. He let his eyes stay on the screen, watching as the black ship grew. It was hard to see— but there were a lot of stars beyond it, and it blocked those off as it passed; also, even the blackest black paint couldn't be as dark as raw space, and its outlines showed dimly.

They were within a hundred miles of the ship when it first seemed to notice them. It was Anderson who caught the trouble, and pointed it out. The black ship was no longer growing; it was actually getting smaller!

Then they all saw it. The ship ahead began to shrink rapidly. In a minute it was half the size it had been. Hoeck blinked, and punched feebly at the calculator suspended above his horizontal seat. His voice was unbelieving. "Acceleration over fifty gravities!"

Such a burst of sheer drive should have crushed flat any life inside in seconds. It would make a normal man seem to weigh over four tons! And no ship in the Solar Federation Navy could do better than ten gravities of acceleration, even for a second.

Commander Griffith cut their own acceleration to a minimum, until their weight seemed no greater than it had been on Mars. "Prepare proton rifle!" he called.

"Proton gun ready." The reply came back at once.

Griffith called down the co-ordinates of the other ship's location. It was a tiny thing now, but still visible in the radar screen. "Fire!" he ordered, when the co-ordinates were checked.

Almost instantaneously, a terrific burst of fire seemed to erupt in the telescope screen where the black ship had been. Then it faded, and the black ship was a tiny spot, surrounded by a blue haze that turned red and disappeared. Again the proton gun fired, and again. The results were the same.

Something seemed to kick at the *Lance of Deimos*. Bob suddenly was tossed back of his seat as the ship jerked sharply, its nose tilting sharply. The kicks came again, one for each blast that had been fired from the proton gun.

This time it was Bob who took a wild guess, culled out of all the fantastic stories and articles he had read. "Pressor rays!" he gasped. Nobody had ever figured out what tractor and pressor rays were, beyond the fact that they pulled or pushed, but that hadn't stopped writers from speculating on them.

Hoeck snorted, but Commander Griffith nodded doubtfully. "It's as good an explanation as any. Something pushed against us, anyhow—and it wasn't an accident. I might guess some kind of rebound, but the jolts came faster than we fired the proton gun. That was a warning!"

Then abruptly the pip that marked the black ship on the radar screen disappeared. It had been shrinking to a point, but this was different. It was as if someone had drawn a curtain across space, cutting off the ship from them.

Another miracle! Now the ship could neutralize the radar beam. That meant it either had to absorb the beam or become completely transparent to it—and one was as impossible as the other.

"Delayed reaction from the proton blasts," Anderson said doubtfully. "Maybe he blew up."

Commander Griffith shook his head. For the first time Bob could remember, his father looked completely unsure of himself. "No—you know that couldn't explain it. The fragments would show up on the radar just as strongly as the ship did. He just neutralized our beam."

He sat staring at the controls and the screen, obviously hating to give up, and yet with nothing to do.

They couldn't locate the ship; if they did, they couldn't catch up with it. Even if they were right beside it, their best weapons were harmless, while it could play games with them by sending harmless little jolts to tell them to go away and stop being bothersome.

Finally Griffith sighed heavily, and shook himself. "I guess we write ourselves off as failures," he summed it up. "Plot me a course back to the rest of Wing Nine, Hoeck. We'd better stop chasing hobgoblins and get back to our mission."

There was nothing else to do, Bob realized, but it didn't end his disappointment. He'd grown up with the idea that any Navy ship was a match for any number of pirates and one of the favorite games at the Academy had been based on elaborate movements of pieces on a board where all were pirates except one Navy cruiser. Now, in his first encounter, he was going down heavily in defeat—hopelessly outclassed by a single pirate ship.

It wouldn't make a pretty story to tell! And it wasn't good to think about.

Hoeck was just looking up from his calculations when a signal buzzed from the intercom. The Commander pressed down one of the buttons automatically. "Control."

"Sparks," the voice said quickly. "Commander, I've just got another message from the *Ionian!*"

"The *what?*"

"The *Ionian,* sir. It was full of static, but someone was yelling for help and complaining about being stranded by pirates without air. He didn't know the standard code at all, sir, and his power was fading pretty fast." Sparks was obviously doubtful about it himself. "I tried to call back, but I got no answer."

"Could anyone still be on board?" Griffith asked Anderson.

The Leftenant nodded slowly. "I suppose so. It would take days to examine every hiding place there; we just looked in every logical place. But how would he send out a voice message without air?"

"Snap open his helmet, toss in the mike, and close it again. If he held his breath, the suit would fill almost at once, and he'd be unhurt," Bob answered, and again he was borrowing from some of the adventure fiction he had read. "There'd be some leak near the wires, but he could send a message, pull out the mike, and close down tight again."

Griffith nodded approvingly at Bob. "I did it myself once, just to test it. The same story you read, Bob, I'll bet. Sparks, keep sending out assurances—in case his receiver has a light—to tell him we're answering. Hoeck, you'd better give me another course."

"Already done," the navigator said. He passed it over.

This time deceleration was held to six gravities pressure, but it lasted longer. The hulk of the *Ionian* had been drifting along at a constant speed, while the *Lance* had built up to a much higher speed and then drifted on at that greater rate. The distance between the two ships was considerable.

But matching course and speed was routine, now that pirates didn't have to be considered. They snapped out of high drive almost beside the derelict ship, and with only a slight tendency to drift apart. Commander Griffith corrected this with a few quick blasts of the little steering rockets. Through the viewport Bob could just see some of the crew getting the rubbery tube ready to connect the two ships again.

He looked inquiringly at his father as Anderson got ready to go across, and the Commander nodded. This time Anderson was buckling a heavy automatic pistol outside his suit. He gave one to Bob. "We don't take chances. If there's anything funny, shoot first and then get back to the *Lance*; we have to figure it might be a trap."

"I'll cover you from here," Griffith added. His eyes were worried as he looked at Bob, but he made no move to hold the boy back. In the Navy, voluntary risk was expected.

They went cautiously across and through the open port of the air lock. Inside, everything was just as they had left it. Anderson inspected the way carefully, but he seemed satisfied. They turned toward the radio room. If the person making the call had any sense, he'd wait right there until help came.

Going cautiously through the deserted, lifeless passages of the ship began to give Bob a feeling that he'd had before only when he was a kid and had been hearing too many ghost stories. But he repressed it savagely. Then they were in front of the door that was marked with the zigzag symbol of electronics.

Anderson opened it cautiously. There was no air to carry sound, and the sponge-rubber soles of the space suits made no thud that could be carried through the floor. The small figure sitting at the radio desk never looked up.

The light on the panel was blinking in response to Sparks's call, but it apparently had meant nothing. The figure sat slumped forward hopelessly, his helmet buried on his arms, which were resting on the desk. It wasn't until Bob touched him on the shoulder that he stirred.

Then he sprang up as if stung, and swung on them. His eyes dropped to the Navy insignia, and the alarm went out of his face, to be replaced by a sudden wash of relief. He would have fallen if Anderson hadn't caught him.

Bob was shocked himself. He'd expected to find a man but this was only a boy of about his own age. Even through the suit he was short and slim, with a dark skin, black eyes and hair, and almost too handsome a face.

By touching helmets together they could talk, though not very distinctly. The boy obviously had no radio inside his suit, but Anderson bent down and Bob did the same.

The boy was babbling his thanks, but Anderson cut him off. "Are there any more here?"

"No." The boy sounded as if something very unpleasant lay buried in the single word. "No, sir. Only me. Only Juan Román, son of Bartoloméo Román, who was captain of the *Ionian,* and now . . ."

He shuddered, and Anderson nodded sympathetically. It wasn't hard to guess what had happened to his father. Anderson motioned for him to follow and, no longer suspecting a trap, they went back toward the air lock at a faster gait.

The boy looked genuine enough, aside from his obvious condition when they had found him. Io had been settled exclusively by Spanish Americans, and Spanish was the official language there, though most of the people also spoke English. Juan's English contained the faint trace of an accent, and his appearance fitted his obvious ancestry.

Griffith was waiting for them when they came back, standing at the door of the control room. He had tea and wafers waiting for Juan. For a second he seemed surprised at the boy's age, but he covered it quickly, while they introduced themselves.

Then the ship got under way again, heading on the automatic pilot for the rest of Wing Nine. Juan gasped at the pressure of acceleration, but he apparently could stand it. They were not on high drive; probably Griffith had ordered Wing Nine to hold up for his arrival, cutting down acceleration.

"I'll have to ask you several questions," Commander Griffith began. "I know this is no time to bother you, Juan, but I have to get some information."

"I shall gladly give all I can," Juan assured him. "I, too, do not like black ships which come to kill my father."

Although Griffith nodded and smiled, his next question whipped out sharply. "Where did you get your suit, Juan?"

Bob had forgotten that there had been sixty suits in the lockers and only sixty listed on the manifest.

But Juan shrugged. "It was made for me special, because I am too small for a regular suit. When my father let me come on this, my first trip, we ordered it in advance."

Griffith sat back, apparently satisfied, and the rest of the questioning was done more quietly, though it didn't bring as much information as the Commander obviously wanted.

The ship had been carrying drugs to Neptune, as they had guessed. Juan's mother had just died, and his father took him along. He had the run of the ship and was generally enjoying it, before the attack came. Then, out of nowhere—because either their radar was defective or their operator was careless—the black ship had swung in ahead of them. Bartoloméo Román had let out a cry about pirates and had begun, too late, to try to fight back. But at first the black ship had done nothing. It had just hung there in space, keeping half a mile ahead of them, and apparently waiting.

They had sent out a signal, but then something strange happened. The black ship had opened a tiny window, and something blue had floated back to the *Ionian* and straight through the walls into the radio room; after that, the radio was dead. They had waited, too, until his father could wait no more. He had fired his few torpedoes. Then the strange ship had melted their nose and the crew had come aboard.

"And my father, he had put me in my space suit and had made me hide in a closet just beside the control room," Juan finished. "He went to meet them, and I heard him cry out. I wanted to go down, but I could not disobey him. Then there was no air, and I waited and waited. And at last I went to the radio room. The blue stuff was gone then. I called. You came. That is all."

"You never saw the men from the black ship?" Griffith asked, frowning.

"No. Only what I have told you."

Further questioning revealed that Juan had felt the men from the *Lance* moving about—carried as faint sounds through the floor and his suit—but had thought they were still the pirates. Commander Griffith finished at last and sent him down with Anderson to a spare bunk. From the sleepy way he acted, Bob guessed that the tea had held a mild sedative to quiet him down.

"Sound asleep," Anderson reported ten minutes later. Then he glanced out. "Hey, we're back with the Wing!"

Griffith nodded. "We caught up five minutes ago. I wish that boy had seen them!"

"What good would it have done?" Bob asked. "Pirates don't look much different from anyone else, do they?"

"These might—since they're no pirates!" The Commander nodded, sucking thoughtfully on his pipe, a dark cloud of gloom on his face. "No human being designed that ship. And no human science could do what it did. That leaves just one place for them—Planet X! It's inhabited, all right, and by a race of some kind that's centuries ahead of us. I'd like to know what they look like."

He sucked on his pipe again, and frowned more deeply. "Well, we know one thing. Whatever form of life is out there, it's unfriendly and it's dangerous! Maybe too dangerous!"

CHAPTER 5 /

Outpost of Neptune

A LITTLE LESS than two days later they turned over and began decelerating toward Neptune, needing the same time to cut their speed that had been required to build it up. But aside from that and the worry that hung over the ship, there was little for Bob to watch or do.

The tradition of keeping him running errands had been dropped, probably because the Commander was too busy trying to think things through and make his report on Outpost carry the weight he felt it should. At present he was refusing to radio problems of the situation ahead, on the grounds that information might be picked up by people outside the Fleet, which would lead to a panic that could only cause harm.

Bob spent most of the time with Juan Román. The boy seemed to have buried his grief somewhere deep inside himself, and to be resigned to whatever happened. He was strangely serious and naïve, with little of the gaiety for which his people were famed. This may have been partly due to his recent tragedy, but Bob had the feeling that much of Juan's seriousness was basic to his character.

He obviously didn't want to talk about his past, and Bob and the others respected his wishes. With a somewhat reluctant permission from Bob's father, they wandered about the ship. There Juan showed an amazing ability to pick up details quickly. He admitted that he had wanted to be an engineer and that he had spent

41

most of his time as a boy hanging around the shops where the big freighters were repaired. But Navy ships were different, and he absorbed everything he saw.

Ten days after taking off from Mars they landed on the little moon of Neptune known as Outpost. Scarcely two hundred miles in diameter, it circled the big planet at a distance of five million miles. It was the farthest port of the Space Navy, more than two and one-half thousand million miles from the sun, and usually staffed with the minimum number of men and ships. But now, with the expedition to Planet X scheduled from there, and with the pirates active throughout the outer planets, it was filled.

The big dome of the landing field opened for Wing Nine, and they found hangar space reserved for them, as well as a celebration, which Griffith at first started to cancel, but changed his mind. Stopping it would cause more comment than anything else, while a few wild tales of a remarkable pirate from the crews would be put down to nothing more than their imaginations.

Housing for the officers was provided at the edge of the field, just beyond the dome that covered it. Here there was no air, of course, and any air would have frozen solid, in any event. Plastic domes covered everything, with passages connecting them together into a sprawling city of bubbles.

Commander Griffith installed Juan and Bob in their quarters in his apartment and then disappeared on the official report he had been sweating out during the trip. He was hardly gone before Simon Jakes knocked on their door. He looked tired and drawn, but about as close to being happy as Bob had ever seen him. To Bob, remembering the grueling drive at top cruising acceleration, he looked like an illusion; he couldn't possibly be on Outpost.

"Surprised to see me?" he asked needlessly. "I told you the *Icarius* had heels. Got here yesterday, and been waiting for you. Hey, who's he?"

Bob introduced Juan, with a quick and careful account of how he happened to be along. Simon shook his head and Juan's hand. For his part, Juan seemed to see nothing ridiculous in the appearance of Jakes. Simon must have sensed it, for he softened and relaxed a little in the general introductory conversation, while Bob's curiosity continued to grow.

Finally, Jakes grinned again, and got back to the subject. "I came at a straight four gravities, except for a few rest hours. I brought a letter from your mother, too. Never thought I could take that kind of pressure, did you?"

"I still don't," Bob answered flatly. Then something flashed into his mind from their few talks while Jakes had been at the Academy. "Your liquid cushion!"

Simon swelled out more than ever, nodding vigorously. Pride made him look more foolish than ever, but at that moment he didn't mind his appearance. "That's it. I got it—a seat made of a new elastic and filled with salt water, just about the same density as my body. When the pressure builds up, I sink into it—except that I wear a mask that lets me see out. Liquid equalizes pressure in all directions. And I can really pile on the pressure. Your precious Navy's already radioed Outpost—after I had Dad give them the dope and they checked my time—and they want my invention. And I'll bet now they let me go along to Planet X!"

Bob didn't have the heart to disillusion him about his present chances of reaching Planet X. If Simon had finally done what no one had succeeded in doing—even with the help of a new plastic elastic—he deserved a little boasting. Bob couldn't help wondering, though, how many experts had been hired by the Jakes family to do the real work on the problem.

Tired as he was, he went along to inspect the new seat, with Juan trailing them. It was simple enough in principle. By sinking down into the elastic-covered liquid, the pressure was equalized on all sides, instead of merely trying to force a man's stomach flat against his backbone. But the metal framework and suspension that made the chair possible was a mechanical marvel, as was placing of the controls so that they could slide back with the hands.

"How about a demonstration?" Jakes wanted to know. He brushed aside the protests that Bob started, and switched on the radio to the field control. "Jakes in the *Icarius*," he announced. "I'm going on a test run."

The monitor's voice was polite but firm. "Sorry, Mr. Jakes. Outpost Field is quarantined—full security blanket. You are not to leave the field without the permission of Commander Jergens *and* Commander Griffith! Repeat. Don't leave the field! Violations will be punished as acts of treason!"

Jakes sputtered, but the radio went dead. He shook his head and finally gave up, trailing the other two as they moved off the field. Bob knew that it meant his father had convinced Outpost Commander Jergens of the origin and meaning of the black ship. By now the ether must be burning with a carefully coded account going back to Mars and to Earth. Naturally, though, it would be kept from the public as long as possible, and no one would be permitted to leave Outpost, where the secret might leak out.

"Come on, Si," Bob volunteered. "Might as well go back to my place and I'll treat you to dinner. Dad won't be home until late, I suppose."

In that he was wrong. His father was sitting in the little living room, with another man, whom Bob recognized as Commander Jergens. The man looked older, thinner, and more uncertain than ever. His sandy hair and mustache went with a drooping expression that made him look like something out of one of the old British comedies—the absent-minded, doddering Lord Somesuch-or-Other.

Commander Griffith spotted Bob and Juan first, and waved them in. "Here are the boys. We can go ahead, though—they know as much as I do, and they can keep their mouths shut." Then he saw Jakes, and frowned slightly.

But Jergens motioned Jakes in quickly. "Simon Jakes—son of my old friend Roger Jakes. Brilliant mind. Made a big contribution, you know, the seat they're installing on the Fleet at Mars. Went to the Academy, before he took up inventing. Very high recommendations from Earth."

Commander Griffith stuck out his hand. "Hello, Simon. Quite a trip you made; it beats the record. We've met before, you see, Commander."

"Oh!" Jergens seemed somewhat disappointed, but he rallied quickly. "Well, small universe, as I always say. But you know, you can't very well exclude him now—not if your boy and this other know. Not after all Mr. Jakes has done for the Navy."

Griffith's mouth twitched faintly, but he nodded. "If I know boys, he already has enough information to find out the rest; as soon as a boy finds there's a secret, he has to ferret it out. Okay, Bob, fill in the details for Simon. You might do it over the dinner I had sent up—out in the dining room."

He turned to Jakes then, estimating the other carefully. "I'll be honest with you, son. You're something of a fool, and you've got a hero bug you'd be better off without; I know your Academy record. But I think you're also able to keep your word, and as honest as most of us. What Bob will tell you is the top military secret of the system. I want your word you won't discuss it with anyone except those present, and then only in private. Not even to your best friends and business acquaintances. Do I have that word?"

"Yes, sir. You have it." Simon had straightened to as good a parade-dress stand as the Academy had been able to drill into him. He met the older man's eye, and then smiled. "Thank you, sir. And—and thanks for putting it that way, sir."

Bob tried to listen to what the two Commanders were saying while he filled the amazed Jakes with the facts. But he needn't have tried. The conversation was still going strong when they went back to the living room.

"We've decided to make you and Juan ensigns for the duration of the emergency," Bob's father told Jakes. "That puts you under Navy officer regulations. You'll both be quartered here with me." Jergens frowned faintly at that, but let it go. "And you're both on indefinite leave, at once. That is, if you'll accept the oath?"

Jakes nodded quickly, and Juan gave his own quiet assent, with the touch of a smile around his lips. He seemed somewhat amused at the idea, though Bob couldn't see why. Maybe those from a merchant planet like Io thought all the rules and regulations of the Navy ridiculous, as many other civilians did. Griffith administered the oath quickly, and made out two handwritten slips of paper.

"Bob," he said then, "you're automatically Navy, but we're raising you to the rank of ensign at once, without leave. All right, boys, relax. It's probably better having you listen in than trying to find any privacy in that madhouse Jergens calls headquarters; we tried that this afternoon. Now, where was I?"

"You said the piracy . . ." Jergens began.

Griffith nodded. "Thanks. No, I don't think all that piracy we've had comes from Planet X. I think not more than three of the attacks show any signs of it. That one a month ago near here, that freighter the miners saw towed off just afterward, and this job with the *Ionian*. The rest are just a bunch of the usual crooks capitalizing on a sensational crime; we always get that. And the more reports there are, the more fools will try piracy instead of honest shipping. I don't think any culture having the power of Planet X would bother with regular piracy."

"Might be war, you know. Undeclared. Maybe don't know a warship from a freighter. Just downright nasty, maybe," Jergens suggested.

"Nonsense. Any race that has advanced that far has advanced enough to know that nastiness and war aren't worth the trouble. Look at us; we fought some bitter wars while we were getting started with our technical development. But the further we went, the harder it was to start a war. Oh, once it started, it was a huge one. But after we had power enough from the atom, and room enough on the planets, war began to die a natural death. We almost had one a hundred years ago—but two hundred years back we *would* have had one. Now people get around too much to hate other people, and there are too many good things which war would destroy. So we don't have wars."

"Another culture might," Jergens objected. "Anyhow, they jumped the *Ionian.* I say we have to attack now."

Bob's father filled his pipe, mulling over his ideas. "I don't believe they really did attack, Commander. From what I saw and what Juan said, they just hung in space ahead of the *Ionian* and tried to keep her from communicating—harmlessly. It wasn't until Román sent the torpedoes against them that they hit back. And the same with me; they had the stuff to take me, I'd guess. But all they did was bat me around a trifle and vanish. I think we should try to make peace, if possible, before going in blindly. Send a single official scout out, if you like, but try to come to terms with them."

Talk went on, far into the night, without much result. At first Bob had been surprised by his father's stand, but on looking back he saw that the black ship apparently hadn't done any attacking. He grew more convinced as his father developed his case, and he noticed that Juan was silently nodding agreement.

Jergens didn't really argue. His one stand was that they couldn't tip off the enemy that he was known; they had to wipe him out at once, before he knew his secret was discovered. Otherwise—and this seemed his real worry—Outpost might be wiped out at any time; and, of course, the other planets later.

"I'm not trying to deny your ideas," Griffith pointed out finally. "I just don't think we can decide here. This is too big. All I want is a chance to use your encoder and transmitter and get in touch with some of the men at Fleet Headquarters."

Jergens looked distressed, and pulled at his drooping mustache. "Wish I could, Griffith. But you know the encoder's assigned for administrative use. Operations Fleet uses a different type code. Against the rules to let you have this one. Tell you what, though." He brightened suddenly. "Write it up, list the men you want it to reach, and I'll try to send it out first thing. Cuts the Gordian knot, eh? Always a way, I always say, without breaking rules."

Bob's father seemed dissatisfied, but he agreed. Then the meeting broke up. "Do your best," were Griffith's last words as he headed toward his typewriter.

"Think he will?" Bob asked, when the man was gone.

His father shook his head. "Maybe. Jergens is scared for Outpost, though, and all wrapped up in red tape. But I can't stand by while we get mixed up in a war we may very well lose without appealing to the men who have some sense. I still say that ship could have wiped out the *Lance* without half-trying—and it didn't. That's the one hope I can see in this mess."

During the next week Bob hardly saw his father. He knew the Commander was trying to make sure the story got through and to cut all the red tape that might be holding it up. He also knew that it had to be done without infringing on the authority of Commander Jergens.

The three boys talked the matter over incessantly. As Bob had guessed, Juan agreed that peace should be tried. He was disgusted to find that Jakes couldn't see it. Simon was all for attacking at once.

"If they're so strong, that makes us savages," he claimed. "And a civilized culture always takes over savages. Me, I'd rather go down fighting than have them push us aside because they had better weapons. Anyhow, where'd they get the weapons? Fighting, that's where! All this peace nonsense makes me sick. Peace— you mean surrender! If I can find a way, I'm going to slip out to Planet X and do a little spying. And if I get back, I'll bet I have proof of what they mean to do."

Bob could only shake his head and hope that his father succeeded. But he had his doubts. And it turned out quickly enough that the doubts were justified.

Nine days after the *Lance* reached Outpost, the whole Outfleet strength of the Navy came down in wave after wave of ships, overflowing onto the frigid surface beyond the dome. Bob counted the groups of huge battleships and felt sick inside.

There could be only one answer. Whether because Jergens had sent only a prejudiced account, or because his father's friends had failed, it seemed that the Solar Federation had decided on a full invasion of Planet X. They were going to try the old, hopeless trick of seeking peace by wiping out the other side!

CHAPTER 6 /

Unnatural Orbit

SIMON JAKES SHOULD HAVE BEEN PLEASED. As it turned
out, the Outfleet had made the long trip at the unheard-
of steady acceleration of better than five gravities of
pressure and had done it in less than seven days. Bob's
father broke that news when he came home, looking
worn and unhappy.

"Your father must have been making up seats for
months, Simon. As soon as you broke the record and
this news got back, he was able to ship enough to Mars
under emergency high-drive to outfit every ship there.
You'll be listed as a boy genius, a patriot, and probably
as the richest young man in the world. I gather he's
making a nice profit for you."

"He can't!" Jakes was on his feet, his hands clenched
until the knuckles were white. "I told him. I told him
I'd done half of the work on this when I was in the
Academy. I built the first model there. Even if it failed,
that makes the idea Federation and Navy property.
Look, sir, I never wanted the money. I've got money
enough. I wanted it assigned to the Navy. Honest!"

Griffith nodded slowly, managing a touch of a smile.
"I believe you, Simon. And I'm glad you felt that
way—though I suppose your father really did us a
service, as it turns out. Well, we'll let the courts decide
on the patents. I hear the Fleet Commander has promised you an interview and a favor, as a result of the way
those acceleration seats worked. Is that right?"

Jakes nodded, while Bob looked up in surprise. He was amazed that Simon hadn't bragged about it, until he began to suspect the reason. "A captaincy! Your father's arranged for you to get a courtesy rating as captain so you can go with the Fleet!"

Jakes nodded again, and his face flushed. He knew what Bob and all Navy men thought of anyone who managed to get a rating through pull, even for services rendered to the Navy.

Bob's father shrugged and turned toward the little room he used as an office. Simon fidgeted, and then blurted out a rush of words. "Okay, okay. I guess I know what you think. I'll start packing."

It was something that hadn't entered Bob's mind, and he saw the same surprise on his father's face. "Jakes," the older man said quietly, "I want an apology for that. I invited you to share these quarters because you were a friend of Bob's. All I asked was that you behave while here. I don't throw a man out because I happen to disagree with him about his own private affairs."

Simon hesitated, and then dropped his eyes. "I—I guess I got out of bounds. I'm sorry, sir, but—well, I'm sorry. And they can keep their blamed captaincy! Sir?"

He hesitated longer this time, after Griffith had nodded permission for him to go ahead. "Well, Simon?" the Commander finally asked.

"Well, I just wanted to know why you questioned me in the first place?"

Griffith dropped into a chair and began stuffing his pipe. "I guess you have the apology coming this time, Simon," he began. "I was out of bounds myself. I was trying to use you!"

"Sir?" This time sheer surprise filled Jakes's voice. Griffith nodded, and puffed out a slow cloud of smoke.

"That's right," he said. "You see, I failed to get a chance to see the Fleet Commander. Wallingford's aides said he was too busy; he was in conference with Jergens. I had no idea that you were convinced of the necessity for war, and was hoping you'd get me an audience, together with Bob and Juan. I don't usually go in for such maneuvers, but in this case it's important enough to try anything."

"You know then that I think we *should* attack," Simon said.

"I know. I was planning a long speech about how we'd taken you in and made you one of the family, and about fair play—all that sort of thing. As I said, I was stepping out of bounds myself. I hadn't thought it through. I was simply planning to take advantage of being your host—which is a lot worse than throwing you out would have been. Let's both forget it, shall we? It's time we turned in."

Simon gulped out something. He was still standing there when Bob and Juan went into their room. Then they heard the door of his little room close softly. For a minute Bob had hoped that Jakes was going to be generous enough, on something besides money, to give his father what he wanted. Bob finally fell asleep, wishing he knew some way to help. Maybe in the morning he could talk with Jakes.

But Simon was already gone; the Fleet Commander's car had apparently called for him early. Bob's father looked as if he hadn't slept, but he seemed more cheerful as he sat reading the notes he had typed out.

"Unofficially, the attack's due to take off from here day after tomorrow," he told Bob. "That's unofficial, as I said. The official statements claim that they are conferring on the question of whether Planet X is an enemy or not, but that was decided before they even got here. Jergens never sent my reports, of course, and he's closed every chance I have to appeal, he thinks."

He put the papers in his brief case, and began to button his jacket. "Better get a move on, boys. I'll want you to testify."

The phone rang almost as he finished, before Bob could ask the obvious question. Griffith picked it up, and the smile on his face deepened. "Yes? . . . Yes, sir! . . . In fifteen minutes!"

He was whistling softly as he hung up. "Simon's face gave him away this morning," he said casually. "I guessed that he'd changed his mind."

"But why?" Bob asked.

His father shook his head. "I can only guess. He's a lot more complicated than you'd think, Bob. But it was partly because he felt it would win our approval, and he wants approval pretty badly; partly, I suppose, because it looked like the grand and noble gesture. It doesn't matter. We can't spend our time analyzing our friends. We have to take them as they are. You ready?"

The car was waiting as they came out, and the way was cleared straight through to the Fleet Commander's office in a hastily converted hangar. This time, the aides rushed Griffith and the two boys in at once.

Admiral Wallingford stood up and came around his desk with an outstretched hand. "Griffith! Hey, you're filling out! Used to be just a gangling kid when you served under me on the old *Lance of Arcady!* I suppose this is your boy, Bob? Right. And Juan Román. Quite an adventure you had. I've been wanting to meet you."

He sounded completely sincere, and Bob noted that his father was now relaxed and smiling. "It didn't seem that way yesterday, Admiral! I even tried to send in a private message to joggle your memory, but your flunkies wouldn't have it."

Wallingford nodded. "So young Jakes was telling me. Crazy kid! Actually told me what I could do with his captaincy—not that I'd have commissioned him anyhow, though I expected to have to restore him at the Academy, or some such. But I was grateful when he told me you'd had trouble, so I upped that phony ensign rating you gave him to Junior Leftenant for the duration, with indefinite leave. Then I called in my aides and told them what would happen the next time they pulled a trick like that. I got so worked up I near forgot to call you. Anyhow, what can I do for you, young man?"

He sat back quietly as Commander Griffith ran through the outline of his arguments, handing over the papers that held a more detailed account. When it was finished, he nodded, and turned to the two boys.

He was still pleasant, but Bob was soon sweating under his cross-questioning. Just what *had* they seen when they came up to the *Ionian* and the black ship, anyhow. Under the merciless questions, he began to realize that nothing had been very definite; the view in the screen had been bad; and they'd only come in on the tail end of the whole business. He found himself pouring out his theory that it had all been a fake, and was almost ready to believe it again.

"Good idea," Wallingford approved. "I like that. Wouldn't stand up, of course, but no man should ever forget that somebody may just be trying to trick him. Go on, what about your vision under high-drive while you were watching the black ship run away? Sure you weren't too busy with your theory to concentrate?"

When Wallingford had finished questioning Bob, he reviewed it all again, and then started in on Juan. There he stopped and did a quick double-take. Juan Román remained as quiet as ever under his questioning, but each question brought forth an answer that took care of it completely, nailed it down, and tied the answer into all that had been said before.

Wallingford held up his hands. "Look, suppose you just tell me everything. Then, if I have any question, I'll ask them. If you take that long about everything I ask, we'll never get done."

When Juan was finished, the Admiral considered silently. "Sounds pretty complete," he admitted. "Only I understand you didn't use emergency code. Do you mean to say your father was a merchant captain and you never picked up that information about shipping?"

"I picked it up, yes," Juan admitted levelly. "But after I got the microphone inside the suit, I thought if I didn't use it, anyone hearing me would know there was no regular crewman or officer there to send the message. And they would be more concerned and come faster. They would not first stop to ask long details, like who was captain, and what registry, and how long could I hold out. Also, I knew help was coming by the light that flashed. I was not despairing for myself. I was unhappy because help could not come to my father."

Wallingford shook his head slowly, staring at the boy. He blinked again. "Never would have thought of not using code like that, would you, Griffith? Well, I think I can say I believe your story. But what can I do about it?"

"Stop this stupid attack until we can find out what the race on Planet X is like!" Griffith suggested quickly.

"Maybe. You've got a lot of truth and wisdom on your side. None of us, except addlebrains like Jergens here, wants war. If you're right—and I suspect you are, pretty much—we stand a good chance of being wiped out. On the other hand, maybe we can't risk peace. A culture superior to ours in strength and weapons might simply enslave us. Besides, it's strange that with such ships they haven't tried reaching the inner planets, where their own peace suggestions are thickest. If we can't trust them—and this is still debatable—then our only hope is a quick attack in full strength."

"Does that mean I've failed?" Bob's father asked.

"No." Wallingford considered it carefully. "No, you've done all you can. You've convinced me I should take this matter up with the staff back on Mars. But I don't think we can change their minds now, to be honest about it. If the full account had reached them first, they might have gone slower. But they've pretty much made up their minds. So have the top circles of the Federation government, and it takes a lot to unmake those minds. The very idea of an alien race in the Solar System—one with ships and weapons—scares them. It's only recently that we've stopped being afraid of our own kind, that we've quit fighting amongst ourselves;

you can't expect us to trust any other race yet. Look, I'll do everything I can, and promise nothing. Fair enough?"

Commander Griffith nodded. "All I expected, really."

"Good, then that's settled. Now get out of here, before I get further behind in my work." Wallingford chuckled, and reached for the pile of papers in front of him. He looked up, just as the others reached the door. "Dinner's at seven, young man, and my wife will want to meet you again. Wish I could invite the boys, but we're cramped for space. I'll send the car around." Then he buried his head in his work again.

Commander Griffith was dressing for the dinner when Simon Jakes finally came in. For some reason he seemed uncertain and more awkward than usual. Bob looked up quickly, and was surprised when his father paid no particular attention to Jakes. He adjusted the tie that he could have fixed perfectly with one hand, untied it, and studied his face in the mirror.

"Know how to tie one of these things, Simon?" he asked. "I'm out of practice."

Simon brightened. "Sure, sir. Here." His fingers were no longer awkward as he made a neat knot and pulled the ends out to just the right degree.

"Thanks," Griffith told him. "Oh, yes—thanks for passing on the word I wanted to see the Admiral. We had quite a session, and he's agreed to take things up with the staff—though he thinks nothing much will come of it. Think I look good enough to dine with him tonight?"

Simon inspected him carefully, and nodded, beaming. "You look good enough to dine with the President, sir!" he answered.

Bob's father picked up his cap and headed for the door, winking quickly as he passed his son. Bob tried to figure it out, and gave up, but it was obviously the right way to handle things. Jakes was whistling as he followed the other two out to the nearest restaurant. He sat quietly most of the evening, saying nothing about his day and asking nothing about theirs.

They were all in bed when Commander Griffith returned, and still asleep when he left in the morning. Bob found a note that said only the usual, "See you later," and knew that his curiosity would have to wait. Probably no business had been discussed anyhow. The three spent the day watching Wing Nine ships having the new acceleration seats installed; spares had been sent along with the Outfleet for them. It seemed to restore Simon to his old self. He watched the preparations of the whole Fleet with unhappy eyes, grumbling to himself.

"Sucker," he finally said. "Just a natural sucker, that's me. No reason I shouldn't be on one, except being a fool! Well, I can still take the *Icarius* up. Bet I'll learn more than the whole Fleet."

"Bet you'll be shot down before you get there," Bob told him. "Why don't you forget it?"

Jakes grumbled a bit more, and then moved off alone toward his little ship, now almost lost on the crowded field. When Juan and Bob started back to the apartment, he was not around, and was still missing by the time Bob's father returned. But they forgot Jakes as they saw the Commander's face.

He gave them the news at once. "It's not all good, but Wallingford had the attack delayed. Wing Nine takes off tomorrow morning for Planet X, on a scouting mission. We'll land if we can do so. If that looks impossible, we'll try to contact X. We'll try to come back, if that's cut off. All of that peaceably! But we're also under orders to attack at the first sign of trouble; experts are souping up our proton guns to about five times the strength right now. You might call us the defusing squad—either we pull out the fuse and keep Planet X harmless—or else we get blown to bits, while the Fleet tries to figure out what they're up against!"

"But . . ." Bob started to protest.

His father cut him off. "I think it's worth the chance,

Bob. Wing Nine volunteered for the trip to Planet X."

"Then you'd better change your mind, sir," Jakes said from the doorway. They all swung toward him, but he slouched in and refused to meet their eyes. "You know what Planet X is doing now? It's playing space-ship—it's on an unnatural orbit, turning itself right off the course plotted for it. And it's heading in for the or-bit of Earth!"

"There's no such news," Bob challenged him.

"Not officially," he admitted. "I spent the whole af-ternoon buttering up to old Smedley at the observatory here, playing chess to soften him up. He's a chess fiend—and I'm pretty good at it. Here are his figures and the plotted orbit. They'll be official as soon as he checks them once more—probably two days from now!"

Even Bob's father nodded slowly. Dr. Smedley was something of a character and a hermit, which was why he'd come here. But he was probably the best man on orbits in the Federation.

CHAPTER 7 /

Against Planet X

BOB WAS STILL RUBBING the sleep out of his eyes the next morning as he came onto the field and approached the *Lance of Deimos*. Others had been up for hours, going over the rough figures and the projected orbit which Jakes had copied hastily while the old astronomer had been studying his next chess move.

It had been hard to imagine why Jakes had decided to pump the old man, just as it was hard to imagine his being good enough at either chess or at "buttering up" to get the information. But the information on the sheet of paper had an authentic note. Apparently Smedley had been spending all his time studying Planet X. He had the advantage of being two thousand million miles nearer than any other trained observer. He had found a steady change in the orbit, had plotted it, and then checked it with later observation.

According to that, Planet X was heading inward to strike the orbit of Earth, and gaining speed every day. Whatever race was on, it must be driving the whole planet, just as men drove their spaceships, though at considerably less acceleration!

Jakes had claimed he had a headache after the chess session, and had gone to bed. But Bob, Juan and Commander Griffith sat up trying to find a flaw in the figures, without success. They'd spent more time trying to see how it affected their plans and the value of the flight by Wing Nine, with no decision.

The little line moving up the ramp of the *Lance of Deimos* grew shorter. The checker took Bob's card and stamped it with only a casual inspection, and Bob breathed easier. He hadn't been told not to come; nor had he received orders to accompany the scouting trip. Apparently his father had forgotten that Bob was supposed to be part of the Wing.

He killed time by putting his few belongings into his little bunk room until it was only a few minutes before take-off. Then he went up quietly to the control room and dropped into the soft acceleration seat that had replaced the older version. His father glanced up, and turned.

"How'd you get here?" he asked sharply.

"Showed my card and was checked in like the rest of your crew. You informed me Wing Nine was taking off this morning, sir, and I'm reporting for duty!"

For a second, something that might have been pain and fear flickered across Griffith's face. Then a taut smile replaced it, and there was pride in his slow nod. "Quite right, cadet. There can be no favoritism here. Glad you're aboard."

Anderson nodded cheerfully, and even Hoeck managed the ghost of a smile. They looked tense, but with excitement and expectation rather than fear. Bob hadn't thought about being afraid, until then; surprisingly, he was not. He had the curious feeling that nothing too bad could happen to him in the *Lance of Deimos*. He knew it was nonsense, but it was pleasant nonsense. In another ship he'd probably have been scared stiff.

Blast-off was at a full five gravities of acceleration. It was Bob's first experience with the new seats and he was amazed at how much difference they made. They couldn't completely compensate for the pressure, since he had to be free to move, but it was easier to take five gravities with them than three without.

Outpost dropped behind sharply and was soon lost to sight. Ahead lay Neptune. They swung around the big planet, coming fairly close and letting its pull turn their course toward the place where Planet X would be. Bob noticed that Hoeck had based his course on the orbit Jakes had gotten from Dr. Smedley, and not on the predictions of the official Navy computer.

Then general call sounded in his radio, and he saw his father busy at the microphone. He was telling the personnel of all the ships everything that he had been able to find about the invading planet, including the fact that its orbit was believed to be changing. Most of what he had to say, they had partly learned before, but he obviously hadn't wanted to brief them while they were still on Outpost. Rumors were not the same as official information to the men.

When his father had finished, the automatic pilot was on and there was little to do in the control room. Anderson's voice sounded more relaxed, though only his eyes and hands showed through the skin of the seat. "I still don't see how any race can live out that far from the sun," he said. "Temperature must be about absolute zero."

"They'd have to have some way of warming the planet," Bob's father answered. "No real science could develop without heat to handle metals. Any planet which can maneuver like a spaceship has a culture too advanced to suit me."

Bob had his own puzzle. "But how did they escape discovery so long, then?" he wanted to know. "All right, maybe they were too far out for spotting by telescopes before this. But if they were traveling around in their ships, there should be some account of them."

Griffith nodded. "I heard an unofficial statement that some scientists think the planet doesn't belong to the sun at all. It may have somehow gotten loose from another star and come clear across space to us. In that case, we didn't run into this race before because it's just arriving in this section of the universe."

"Which would make it even harder to see how they kept it warm," Anderson said. "Atomic power would work for a while, but eventually they'd run short of power. At the speed they're making, it would take thousands of years to cross from the nearest star to the sun."

There were no answers to these questions. Their only hope of finding out was in the faint chance that they would be able to land on X and somehow establish communications. But even Griffith wasn't too optimistic. If the planet was deliberately swinging down to Earth's orbit, it didn't look like too friendly a move.

The ships of Wing Nine went on piling up speed. The seats still worked perfectly, but they had one major disadvantage—a man couldn't leave them to do anything beyond his immediate reach. Oh, he could stagger a few steps and back, but not enough to be of any use in a possible battle. That would still have to be fought at lower acceleration.

They were already decelerating when Planet X first began to show up on the screen of the telescope. It was a world slightly smaller than Earth, but a mere point on the screen.

"Right where Smedley's orbit put it," Griffith commented. "That seems to prove his theory."

Bob would have been happier if Smedley had been wrong; his faith in the *Lance* wasn't quite so strong as he stared out at the impossible planet toward which they were heading.

Hour by hour, it swelled in the screen. Nobody commented when the first sign of clouds showed up. They had known that somehow it had to be a planet warm enough for that—even though heat couldn't possibly reach them from the sun, which lay over four thousand million miles away and was no more than a bright star on the screen.

It looked like a peaceful world though. The clouds were soft and fleecy, and there were signs of continents and seas below them. Like Earth, this planet seemed bluish-green from space, adding to the appearance of familiarity.

"Commander!" It was Anderson's voice, suddenly

sharp. He had stretched out a hand to point at one section of the screen. "Ships!"

They were tiny specks on the screen, perhaps a hundred of them. But they were in a flying-wing formation, and were moving rapidly. There was no mistaking the fact that it could only be a military force.

"They still might be peaceable," Griffith said, but he sounded doubtful. "Try to contact them."

Anderson took over the radio controls, by-passing Sparks, and there was a long, tense wait as the radio beam traveled out across the long distance separating the two groups. Then the answer came back. The *Lance* bucked faintly, as she had done in the encounter with the black ship. Anderson tried again, and again the ship received a backward jolt. This time it was followed by a blazing sphere of blue fire that sprang up fifty miles ahead of the ships and suddenly exploded. Another jolt was followed by another explosion at the same distance.

"Ultimatum," Griffith guessed. "Either we go back, or we get that thrown at us. They speak pretty plain language down there!" He punched the intercom quickly. "Bombardiers, ready your lithium bombs!"

These were the most feared weapon of the fleet, and it spoke volumes for the fears of Earth that Wing Nine should have been equipped with the deadly things. Ten of them would be enough to make any world uninhabitable.

"We'll pass right through them," Anderson commented. He was licking his lips now, and Bob found that his own were dry. "At our speeds, we won't even see them when we cut through. They can't do much damage."

Griffith made no comment. "All ships on full emergency," he ordered sharply. "Don't attack first. If attacked, observe no restrictions. We may be saved by our speed, but don't count on it!"

There would have been no chance to cut their speed and flee back to Outpost, even if they had tried. Their momentum would carry them near Planet X, even if they used the maximum braking power.

No further threat had come from the black ships, all of which seemed identical with the one they had seen before. They were rushing closer, seeming to leap ahead on the screen. Now they were visible to the naked eye through the quartz viewport. In a fraction of a second they should be diminishing behind Wing Nine.

Suddenly, at a distance of a few miles, they stopped advancing! From full speed ahead, they were instantaneously moving backward to match the speed of Wing Nine exactly, and then seemed to hover motionless in space.

Commander Griffith gasped, and Hoeck's mouth hung open slackly. No amount of power could do that; no metal known could stand the strain, much less living beings inside them. It represented infinite gravities of acceleration—in fact, it was meaningless. All the laws of momentum made it impossible.

"Cut thrust to one gravity," Griffith ordered. "Then wait at your battle stations. No hostile moves without orders! Anderson, try to contact them again."

The black ships matched the change in acceleration at once. They gave no answer to Anderson's signals for a period of perhaps ten minutes.

Then abruptly one of them flashed up to the *Lance*. There was a faint sound of metal on metal from the hull. The air seemed to grow tense, and a faint feeling of strain hit at Bob's body. For a moment his eyes blurred. Then the black ship was leaping ahead to its original position.

But now they were turned around and headed back toward Neptune—and obviously speeding back at the speed they had been making toward X before! Only a fraction of a second had passed, but their speed had been reversed and the whole ship turned about!

Bob had barely time to gasp before the rear telescreen showed black ships swinging the other ships of Wing Nine after them.

Bob's father had grabbed for the microphone, but he was too late. One of the Wing captains had taken that for an attack. The dazzling lance of a proton rifle struck against the black ship, driving its screen up to a blinding blue, and the other ships were instantly following suit.

"Stop it! Cease fire immediately!" Griffith called. But the fury had started, and it was too late to quit.

Now one of the black ships leaped for the Navy ship that had fired first. With it went one of the blue spheres of ball lightning that had been exploded in space. This time it seemed to sink into the Navy ship, leisurely and without fuss. The ship suddenly exploded, leaving only dust where it had been!

Commander Griffith groaned. "Lithium bombs!" he ordered tensely. It was too late now to hold off the battle. All they could do was to hope the dread weapons would end it in their favor.

At close quarters, the result was instantaneous. Fury beyond description blazed out as a lithium bomb hit one of the black ships. And even their screens couldn't take that. The bulk of the Planet X ship seemed to slump and melt in on itself. Bob saw it eaten away in the radar screen; automatic screens had covered all other viewing plates and ports, to keep the fatal radiation out of the Navy ships. Even through airless space, the shock wave of exploding atoms hit the *Lance,* and made her buck under them.

Twenty lithium bombs had been released against the leading Planet X ships. Some targets were duplicated, but seventeen of the black ships disappeared on the first salvo.

The second salvo went off almost as quickly, but some of the black ships were leaping away at impossible speeds. This time less than a dozen of the aliens were destroyed. The rest were now at too great a distance for quick destruction.

But more bombs were on their way. Bright green streaks on the radar screen showed their paths—and suddenly showed them turning over and heading back toward the ships of Wing Nine!

Griffith yanked at the controls, and a full ten gravities of pressure hit at Bob as the *Lance* leaped ahead. Other ships were doing the same, but some had been too slow. They were abruptly caught in the inferno of their own exploding bombs.

There was no time to count damages. Griffith piled on the acceleration steadily, heading back for Outpost. "Full retreat," he was ordering. "Break ranks and separate. Some ships have to get back to base to report!"

One ship from the Wing must have had a foolhardy captain, because another lithium bomb was launched then. From a black ship, a sphere of lightning touched it and exploded it harmlessly. Then more spheres came rushing toward the ships, the black ships diving after them.

Bob had had too much. He buried his eyes by turning his head into the seat, until the explosions were over. When he looked again, the black ships were massed solidly behind them, and there were only three of the twenty Wing ships still operating.

The black ships darted forward in a' solid wall, then halted. But all the fools in Griffith's command had already been killed off. There was no one left to go in for bravado or useless attack on the aliens. The three ships that were left of the Navy forces were all heading homeward at their top acceleration, spreading apart as they went.

The black ships re-formed into another flying wedge and began to fade back toward Planet X.

Bob's father picked up his microphone as he cut the acceleration back to a bearable level. "All ships report," he ordered wearily.

"Carter of the *Mimas Arrow,* here."

"Wolff of the *Achilles Arrow,* here."

"Form up behind me," Griffith ordered them. "And prepare your reports. Radio silence until we reach Outpost. We can't let this leak out."

He cut the connection. His face was worn and old and there was no life in his eyes.

Bob knew how he felt. His own mind was a turmoil of disbelief, fright, misery, and complete hopelessness. They had gone out to try to prevent a war. And now they were going back, completely defeated, to report that the war had already come as a result of their mission.

A war they obviously could never win!

CHAPTER 8 /

Preparation for War

THOUGH NOTHING HAPPENED, the trip back was a nightmare. They didn't bother with rest periods, and there was no conversation in the control cabin. Nobody had the heart to talk. Bob could imagine himself a primitive bushman who had dared make war on a modern world; now he was crawling back to his hut to lick his wounds—not daring to think and not knowing what had hit him.

It grew worse during the next few hours, as the numbness wore off and he began to think and feel the few moments of that horrible battle all over again. Then they had been simply ships exploding; but now came realization that men he had met all his life were simply dust among the stars, gone forever.

There was no consolation in knowing they had also destroyed more of the black ships than they had lost. That had happened only because they had struck when the other ships were unready. And it could never happen again.

Even the original question was unanswered. He didn't know whether the forces of Planet X would have attacked or not; perhaps their trick of turning the fleet had been an attack, and perhaps it had been only an attempt to settle things without war. But from now on, peace seemed impossible.

When they neared Outpost, Bob's father ordered the other two ships ahead of him, and came in in the inverted V that was the ancient symbol of the Fleet that they had failed. But the observers on Outpost must have already known that. Three ships out of twenty returning could never spell success.

There was no crowd waiting for them. The field was deserted, except for military police who were patrolling the borders to make sure no one got through. They landed in the spot reserved for them and went out. Across the field, Wallingford's car waited for Commander Griffith, and patrol cars were lined up for the officers of the three ships. All would have to report in detail.

Bob got through it somehow without cracking. Perhaps it was because he was interviewed last and most of the details were already on record. Wallingford, Jergens, and five other men sat on the panel doing the quizzing. It was not a formal investigation—there was no question of guilt or fault in their defeat. But Jergens' face had a smugness under his newly grown fear that showed the general attitude. If Bob's father had let well enough alone, things would have been different! He was technically in the right, but he would be the black sheep of Outpost, in any event. Unconsciously, people would blame him for starting the war.

Beyond them in the room, a stenographer sat before the keys of the encoder, radioing all details back to Earth and Mars!

It was finally over as far as the officers were concerned. Bob was dismissed, and one of the patrol cars took him to the apartment. He hesitated outside the door, dreading the questioning that would follow. Then he opened it, and found he was wrong.

Juan and Jakes were as sunk in gloom as he was. Juan muttered something and went out to bring him sandwiches and some cold drink. He realized suddenly that he hadn't eaten since the attack. For a moment he tried to shove it away, feeling no hunger.

Jakes scowled at him. "Hey, you eat that, Bob!

Maybe we'll all be dead in another month, but you don't need to starve ahead of time!"

There was no taste to the food, but somehow it made him feel better. Once started, Bob wolfed it down. "I thought you wanted war, Si," he said bitterly.

"Me?" The other stared at him in shocked surprise. "Naw—I'd rather anything else. Just cause I figure we're bound to have it and want to play it the safest way doesn't mean I want it. Why, even Dad doesn't want war—and he could make plenty out of it. Nobody wants war!"

It seemed to be true, from the tone of the local newspaper and the carefully censored radio reports. Nobody wanted war—but the fear of the mysterious Planet X meant they could never avoid it now.

Bob's father came in later. "Help me pack my things, Bob," he requested.

Jakes sprang up before Bob could clear his throat. "You mean . . . They couldn't sack you!"

Griffith smiled wearily. "No, nothing like that. I've been—promoted, is the word they used! I'm now on Wallingford's staff here. It seems I'm the leading expert on Planet X and its ships, and he needs me. Either that, or he's covering me against trouble from Grand Headquarters. But I've been assigned quarters there, so you boys will be on your own."

"Meaning we can't see you—is that it?" Bob asked.

"Something like that. You won't be able to see anyone higher than a Senior Leftenant, I suppose." Griffith began packing his few belongings, hiding his face, but his voice was almost resigned. "You'll have to face it, Bob. For the first time in nearly two hundred years, we're at war. Most of us don't know anything about that—but the real higher-ups haven't stopped studying it, and we'll have to learn to obey them. You boys have no right being on the inside from now on. You'll still have freedom of the town and the old port, of course. But you'll have to act like citizens, not like a private staff. Okay?"

They nodded. War was a mysterious word, but they knew that it kept things from being normal, and they weren't too surprised.

"I'll drop by now and then, when I get a chance. And you all will go on drawing salaries according to your rank, so you'll get by." He put his bag on the floor, and drew himself up. "Attention!"

Juan and Jakes were a little awkward about it, but they managed to come to a ragged attention, together with Bob. Griffith saluted in the almost forgotten formality of the old Navy. "All right. As you were." He picked up the bag and went out.

Bob knew it had been his way of avoiding an awkward scene, but also a reminder that they were now only two phony ensigns and a phony Junior Leftenant, and that they had better learn to act the part.

When he was gone, Jakes stomped about restlessly, muttering; Juan slumped back on the floor. And Bob stood foolishly, without an idea of what to do. Then he shrugged, and slumped off to bed. He heard the others muttering something about another visit to Smedley's observatory, and then heard them turning in. Apparently they felt he wanted to be alone, since Juan went into Jakes's room.

From outside came the sound of lorries driving through the streets and the booming of a public radio that was endlessly recounting the "vicious attack on peaceful ships by the war forces of Planet X." He grumbled and covered his head with a pillow, but it was a long time before he slept.

Jakes came in from outside right after breakfast the next morning, and threw a card on the table. "Got a job," he announced. "Filing down flanges over in the repair shops. They're looking for help."

"Any help?" Bob asked, with a sudden revival of his infrequent respect for the older boy.

"They don't ask questions about age, if you can bur off the flanges. How about you, Juan?"

The Ionian nodded quickly, echoing their feelings.

"Of course. Can we only sit here and twiddle the thumbs? We start when?"

They started at once, it seemed. Workers were being sent from the moons of Saturn as quickly as possible, any workers who could follow orders, together with tremendous quantities of supplies. But Outpost, which had only been a small frontier base, was shorthanded, and would be after they arrived. Plans called for domes to cover the whole area of the little moon. From now on, it would have to be built up to a strength that could safely hold off the possible invading forces of X, and throw forces out to battle on its own.

The work was dull, but that somehow helped. The routine didn't keep them from thinking, but tension was lessened by useful occupation. At the same time, from the shops they heard more of what went on, and saw more of the activities on the field than they would have remaining in the apartment.

The Infleet landed during one of their lunch hours. The blue and gold of Venus, Mercury and Earth were unmistakable. They came dropping from space, spreading even further, until the last ones began to disappear from sight over the horizon. Lorries with airtight bodies ran out to pull off the men, and a constant line of supply trucks began running by the shops where the boys worked. There were more ships on Outpost now than had ever been based at one time on any major planet!

And back in the huge factories of Earth, more were coming off the assembly lines, just as a constant supply of lithium bombs were being made. It was on those that most of the hopes of the Fleet were based. If a few ships could penetrate the lines of the Planet X fleet, and get through to X itself, they might be able to eliminate the whole world.

Meantime, speculation ran high about the absence of attack from Planet X. The more optimistic claimed that this meant that X might have superior ships, but so few that they had to stick to their own planet. The pessimistic claimed that they were waiting for all ships to be based on Outpost, and would then sail in and wipe out all the other planets.

Two weeks after the ill-fated mission to Planet X, the sirens went off wildly in the middle of a work period. Ships were finally sighted and identified as the enemy! The three boys were forced into the stuffy shelter which would be no protection at all if a real attack came, but which gave some feeling of safety to the civilians. They could not make out details from the garbled radio reports at the time, but the crisis was soon over.

Later, they found that three black ships had cruised over, and that ten Wings of battleships had gone up after them. The black ships had waited around, and then simply put on a burst of speed that carried them almost instantly out of sight, down toward Neptune. There was some question as to whether a lithium bomb had destroyed one of them before it disappeared, but it had probably gotten away safely.

Bob and the other two discussed the situation all that night, but there was no real meat for talk. And the next day was their day off, which left them nothing to do. Bob tried to call his father, but found he was in conference with the staff. He went out to take in a show, and gave that up; with the new workers and the whole Navy here, seats were available only on some kind of a black market at prices far beyond his reach.

"We can go over to the observatory," Jakes suggested. "Old Smedley called me up yesterday. He can't find anyone else to play chess with, with this war going on."

Juan stood up promptly and began getting ready, but Bob shook his head. He'd remembered that a letter to his mother was long overdue, and this was the best time to write it. He pulled out his typewriter as soon as the other two were gone, put in a sheet of paper—and stopped.

Plenty had happened, but she already would know everything permitted by the censors. He'd already described his work in the repair shop. And there was literally nothing to say. For the first time, he realized that war was not only frightful; to the man just outside it, it was dull and monotonous!

Maybe that was why war had become unpopular until this new alien world had frightened people into it again. In the old days, men had fought almost hand to hand, and there had been at least the excitement of any good private fight; also, people had been able to get the full picture, and know what was going on. It was almost like a football game. But with advancing technology, an individual became just a dumb cog in a machine so big, he couldn't begin to understand or take any great personal credit. And war lost its neurotic zest.

For want of anything else, he began writing about this idea to his mother, along with the few little personal items he could remember. He stopped to look out into the street and see countless men and women hanging around, having nothing to do once their period of work was over, and he fitted their boredom into his letter.

Then he got up and tore it up. If he ever sent that, his mother would feel sure he was sick and would start worrying twice as much as she would if he didn't write at all.

He went out and bought one of the expensive tissue copies of the Martian *Chronicle,* and tried to read it, since he hadn't seen more than the little local *Post.* But much of the news was meaningless to him. He hadn't followed the current wrangles of the Federation Congress over policy enough to know what they were arguing about.

The editorial pages interested him more. Again he found the curious mixture of fear and eagerness to strike at Planet X and get the suspense over with, and the general dissatisfaction with having to be mixed up in anything as out-of-date as warfare.

Prices were going up on some things. Transportation between planets was being limited. Mars and Earth were blacking out their cities at night. And piracy had increased.

That should have been expected. There were always some people who took advantage of trouble. Another item caught his eye.

Then Bob whistled. It seemed that Simon's father was in trouble; Simon had given the Academy an assignment to his invention of the acceleration seat, and the elder Jakes had patented it without any right to do so. Apparently Simon had been honest in his surprise at his father's actions, and really had been doing the right thing all along.

Bob struggled. He was almost beginning to like the clumsy Jakes, but Simon was such a mixture that there was no way to tell what would come up next. He could do things that required real sacrifice without expecting any credit; and then he could turn around and ruin all his efforts by some stupid and boorish gesture.

Bob went back to try to write a letter, just as the two others came into the apartment. He glanced up to give a casual greeting, and then stopped. Something had obviously happened. The two were no longer bored, and Juan was practically bubbling with excitement.

"You didn't beat Smedley that badly," Bob guessed.

Jakes shook his head. "He beat me—he always does. But Juan slipped in and used his telescope. Not the big one, but the fifteen-inch one with the electronic amplifier. And he found something!"

"On Neptune's side of us . . . a little moon it was, maybe three miles big—half a million miles away. And I didn't tell Smedley, because Simon wanted you to know first, too." Juan's English had a stronger accent than usual.

Bob grinned in puzzlement. "Nothing new about that. Neptune has quite a few of those tiny moons between us and Triton."

Juan nodded. "That I know. But not with the wreck of a Planet X ship upon them. And this one I saw. It was turning around, but I saw it clearly. Lying on a bunch of big white rocks was a black thing, big at both ends, narrow in the middle. And shouldn't I know a ship like that when I see it?"

"Juan came back just when the game was over," Jakes added. "I saw something was up, so we got out fast. As soon as Juan told me about it, we came here on the double."

Bob blinked, slowly digesting this information. If they could get their hands on one of those mysterious ships, and learn how they operated . . .

"How badly broken up, or could you see?" he asked. It would do little good to have only mangled pieces of a ship left over after a lithium bomb had hit.

But Juan shook his head. "Not broken. It was all there, Bob. A whole black ship, just waiting for us."

CHAPTER 9 /

Flotsam of Space

CAPTURE OF A SHIP of the enemy might change the whole picture of the war. Earth scientists couldn't produce the miracles that the Planet X race had, but, once having a ship in their hands, they probably could find out how the machinery worked. Then they would be ahead of the other side, since they'd have their own science, plus that of the aliens—which might prove a great deal more than either had alone.

It would take time, of course; even if they unraveled the secrets quickly, it would require tremendous effort and expense to start the new production and reach an effective level. But there might be ways of stalling for time, and of letting the aliens win hollow victories by carefully planned retreats.

Furthermore, the total population of the Solar Federation was over nineteen billion, which must be more manpower than any single planet could boast. And the total amount of minerals and wealth of resources was bound to be greater than Planet X could have.

Given an equal break on weapons, the Federation would win. And this looked like the break.

Bob wasted no more time on words. He went to the telephone, and began dialing headquarters. If he could get his father on the phone and have him reach Wallingford . . .

Jakes grabbed the phone from his hand. "You aren't

going to call in the Navy, are you, Bob? Hey, what's wrong with you?"

"What else? This is military business, Si—and they're set up to handle it. I want Dad to get this moving, before any time is wasted."

"That's just it—there'll be a lot of wasted time. They'll have to check and recheck—and by now, the ship's probably turned on the other side of the rock. Then they'll have to screen men for good secrecy risks. Heck, by the time all the red tape is done with, the hull could be back here with scientists working on it."

"How? Somebody has to go and bring it in," Bob pointed out.

Jakes nodded quickly. "Sure—we do. We can be there and haul it back in a couple of hours or so. Land it on the other side, where they're working on that improved proton gun; the scientists there can get right to work on it. We'd be back before the Admiral even made up his mind."

"And what will we use to haul it?"

It was Juan who answered this time. "There is Simon's ship, the *Icarius*. It is fast and strong enough to haul from that little world."

"And we could be off Outpost before they even knew we were leaving," Jakes added quickly. "Then, when we had it in tow and were almost back, we could radio our reason for leaving. They'd beef about our going, but they could see what we had from the ground, and they'd be plenty glad to let us land at the right place. We'd use a tight beam, and nobody around here would even know about it, if you're worrying about secrecy."

Bob was tempted. He knew that the proper thing was to turn it over to the authorities, but there was just enough truth in what Jakes was saying to make him hesitate. In handling a large Fleet, the commanding officers did have to run through a lot of red tape for even a simple mission; they couldn't just call in a man and tell him to go and get such and such. Numerous different tiny factors would come up, without the observance of which discipline, logistics, morale and everything else would vanish. Red tape was actually designed to make such matters automatic and hence speed them up; but it took time, in any event.

Besides, after the monotony of the past weeks, the idea was beginning to appeal to him.

"Suppose Planet X is looking for their ship," Simon went on. "Heck, they won't want it to fall into our hands. And they may know it wasn't destroyed. Maybe it sent out a distress signal. So either they are trying to find it or are on their way. We can be there in an hour on top-drive; the *Icarius* will pull better than twelve gravities if we crowd her. But nobody'd be off the ground officially by then."

Juan added his ideas. "And if they see a little ship near by, what do they think? Some little scout, he means nothing. Now if a tug goes out, and they see him, they think he is looking for something to bring back—and that may be their own ship. So they cut him up, after they find where he is going. Obviously, it is much safer to take a tiny ship, like the *Icarius*."

"And suppose they locate the *Icarius* while it's towing back their ship?"

Jakes shrugged. "There's always some risk. There's just less this way."

Bob considered it. The *Icarius* was fitted with four of the acceleration seats, and would store four space suits. Juan was small for one of the standard ones, but he could use it for a while. And in taking off from as light a world as the tiny moon, there would be no major problem; the little ship had power enough, if they handled her gently.

"Do you carry the regular drills, hooks and tow cable for emergency salvage?" he asked Jakes. The other nodded.

It would be a little rugged when they got the prize over Outpost, but by then a tug could be sent up to help. And if they could come close with it, they could even get an air cover from the ships there while they landed. The only risk would be in signaling the ground. They'd see the black ship . . .

No, that wasn't true. They'd spot the light-painted little *Icarius* first, and wouldn't see the black ship against the jet of space until their attention was called to it. A group of scientists out by themselves, away from the main base, would be less likely to fire on them than to listen, anyhow.

"I know enough of the high-priority landing code to get us down all right, I think," Bob admitted. "That looks like the big trouble. Anyhow, if we're spotted taking off, they may train their scopes on us. Then they'll see what we're up to, and may even be ready to help us down."

"See, it's better than I thought," Jakes crowed. "Hey, Bob, I'm glad we waited for you. I was all set to take off, but Juan wanted you along. Let's go."

Bob flashed a quick look of gratitude at the smaller boy. He should have guessed that Jakes hadn't thought of coming to him.

There was nothing which they had to take along, since it would be a short trip, but he picked up his knife and radio on the way out. He'd retuned it to a private band assigned to his father, and it might be handy, in case they wanted to communicate even more privately than beamed general call stuff would permit. He slipped it into his ear and followed them.

It was only a few feet through the tunnel from their dome to the old field where the *Icarius* was parked. Nobody questioned them, since this wasn't reserved territory. Jakes headed for the little ship, grumbling as he saw it had been moved closer to the concrete wall that was the base of the plastic dome. He ran around it, and then nodded.

"It'll be touchy getting her up against that, but I can do it."

Bob took his word for it. Simon'd had another smaller ship before the *Icarius,* and had been in constant trouble for his wild stunting, but he could make a small rocket do tricks. He wasn't as sound as a Navy pilot, but he could probably get out of tighter places.

They piled in and closed the lock. Jakes checked over the supplies and nodded his satisfaction. Then he reached for the controls and pulled them back to a comfortable position from the acceleration chair. Bob glanced up through the viewport, and let out a sudden exclamation.

"The dome! You can't get them to open it for you."

"Don't have to," Jakes said confidently.

The dome was a double plastic shell here. In taking off, a motor snapped the lower dome section open while a ship went through, then closed it. The second dome then opened and closed behind the ship. A little air was lost that way each time, which had to be mined down on frozen Triton, Neptune's biggest and closest moon. But it was all right for a small amount of traffic, and permitted easy unloading of ships within the air-filled dome. The Navy, naturally, found it simpler to land in the vacuum and take the men off in suits.

"You can't crack the dome," Bob protested. "You'd kill half the people inside."

"Wait," Jakes told him. He glanced at his watch, then across the field, where an officer's gig was being filled with fuel. "I figured on that. Jergens goes out to the science base every day on some job. I noticed him before from the repair shop. He'll be taking off in ten minutes."

It was less than that when flame blossomed from the jets of the jig and it began to rise upward. Above, the inner dome began to snap open.

Bob groaned, trying to estimate a speed that would let them escape the closing of the domes without hitting the jib. But Jakes apparently was one of the so-called "natural" flyers. He'd done well in the Academy until they demanded he use instruments. He depended mostly on the feel and what he could see. Now he hit the throttle quickly, cutting on the side rockets to throw the *Icarius* sharply away from the near-by wall.

It was a crazy way to take off, but it worked. They sank back into the seats while the ship jerked upward. Simon hit the braking rockets in the nose, slowing it just before it touched the gig. Then he gunned it forward again. The closing outer dome must have missed them by inches, but his judgment had proved sound enough.

"See what they kicked out of the Academy!" he boasted. Then his face sobered. "Don't say it, Bob. I just can't take routine and discipline. Ten years getting my father to let me go in—and two years getting kicked out in spite of his pull! But I might have stuck it out if all the other guys hadn't hated me for my money. Could I help it if I had private tutors? And don't answer that. Cut off the radio, will you?"

A red light was flashing in the panel before Bob and he cut it quickly. There wasn't much chance they'd be fired on from the ground. The trouble would come when word was sent out and they weren't allowed to land anywhere, except at a military prison for unauthorized departure from a closed port.

"Dad said you might get back in the Academy in a couple more years," Bob told him. Simon swung his face part way around in the mask that held back the cushioning liquid. "That is, if you stuck to rules awhile first."

"Aw. Rules! Like rotting down there and putting this venture through red tape, eh?" Simon's face had grown sour again, and he turned back to his piloting, cutting on the top power of the rockets. It brought a groan from Juan, and the strain told on the other two, but he didn't let up. "Who wants the blamed Academy, anyhow. I'm too old for that stuff."

He was flying by the seat of his pants again, now, and Bob began to wonder how well he had estimated where the little moonlet would be. But he seemed to know what he was doing. He flipped the little *Icarius* over a while later, and began decelerating. It was about the sweetest-handling ship Bob had ever seen; at what it had probably cost, it should have been.

Then the rear screen showed the little hunk of rock coming toward them, right in the cross hairs. It was a feat of navigation that would have made Hoeck blink in surprise. They began slowing down and matching the orbital speed of the moon, which was spinning fairly rapidly on its axis. As they came down, something rose over its steep horizon, and Juan pointed. Without question, it was the hull of a black ship from Planet X.

"No place beside it to land," Simon grumbled. "Guess we'll have to set down up ahead of it. Tow cable will reach, though."

He kicked the *Icarius* around with the steering rockets, and kept coming down without apparent change in deceleration. A high-gravity landing was always dangerous, but he seemed not to know it. Then he flipped the throttle off. They were down, and Bob had hardly felt the contact.

"Sweet," he commented.

"I always make 'em sweet," Jakes answered. "I told you, I'm *good* with a ship. I was going to use this for a racing entry until Planet X came along. Here, you'll find suits in that locker."

Bob began helping Juan into one of them. The smaller boy had trouble with the adjustable straps, and Bob realized he'd probably never really seen a Navy suit before. Then Bob began slipping into another. Jakes was already in his, and was pulling out the heavy drill and towing equipment required to be carried to give aid to a ship in distress, or for seeking aid oneself. The cable was obviously the best grade of silicone fabric, and would stand strain in the cold of space without trouble.

The lock showed the only disadvantage of a smaller ship. It was barely big enough for one to leave at a time, and had to be pumped out carefully after each use. They killed several minutes getting through it.

Juan came out last. "No sign of ships in the radar screen," he reported. "No black ships are following us."

It didn't mean too much, since searchers could have

been on the other side of the little moon, but it was some comfort. The three began to advance carefully over the jagged surface. Here they were so light that a normal step would have bounced them up a hundred feet into space, and have wasted a good many minutes before they floated down. They had switched the suit shoe-soles to automatic grapples, but it still took a good deal of care to travel over the surface of little worlds like this.

They came around a huge, rough boulder finally. Jakes stopped to run the towline carefully along where it would not snag, and then joined the others.

The nose of the black ship lay fifty feet away. It was smaller than the others they had seen, hardly more than three hundred feet in length. But it was an impressive sight here. Bob stirred uneasily as he remembered that there might be living beings still aboard. Then he breathed easier as he saw that it must have struck the surface a terrific blow, since it seemed to have been driven into the rock.

Something looked wrong, though. He moved forward cautiously, and stopped.

The hull hadn't been driven into the ground. It was cut off sharply, just below the center, as if someone had taken a giant cleaver and sliced the ship down one side.

A few feet more, and he knew they had been tricked.

It was no ship, but a mere mock-up. Someone had put it here deliberately, and tried to make it look like a Planet X ship. But it wasn't even built of metal.

It was a thin frame of light metal that rested on the ground. Over that, fabric had been stretched tightly. Bob's hand tore at it, throwing it up out of the way, and he stood looking into what might have been a huge tent.

But it was from Planet X, without much question. The fabric was completely soft, though the temperature must have been near absolute zero. Nobody in the Solar Federation had learned to make stuff like that yet.

CHAPTER 10 /

The Alien Trap

JAKES STOOD BESIDE BOB NOW, staring at the fake ship which had lured them there. "Well, I'll be . . ." It was the first indication Bob had had that these suits were all equipped with built-in radios, though he should have expected it.

"We'll all be," he agreed hotly. "This thing wasn't just put here to improve the landscape. They must have slipped in here with it pretty well ready and put it up while the moon was facing away from Outpost. But it was put here to be seen and to draw a sucker down. It's a trap!"

Jakes muttered to himself. "Yeah," he agreed finally. "And we've sprung it. Now I suppose the hunters are coming to hunt us up. We'd better get back to the *Icarius* fast! Of all the dopey ideas, coming out here for this."

Juan shrugged. "It was your idea, Simon."

"You mean it was yours," Jakes told him angrily. "You didn't yell it out in front of Smedley. You waited until we were alone, and then told me. Naturally I figured you wanted to come for it, and I offered to take you."

"You suggested it, though, Simon. I did, it is true, have the idea. But you were the first to put it into words."

"We're all guilty," Bob said. He was completely disgusted with himself. Wallingford had told him that a

89

smart man always looks suspiciously at strange objects and suspects they might be faked. He knew this himself. But he'd come running here just to get out of the boredom at Outpost—and probably to be a hero, just as Jakes had done!

"We're all guilty together, and we'd all better get out of here before they come," he repeated.

Jakes and Juan started off, and Bob swung to follow them. He tried to hurry over the ground, but something seemed to hold him back. He pushed more strongly, and his feet slipped. With a slow snap, he found himself back where he had been.

The fabric he had touched was more than soft—it was sticky! He'd let go of it, but it still stuck to his space mitten. He picked up a stone quickly and tried to scrape it off, but it seemed to be glued to the metal. "Jakes," he called.

"I'm coming. I saw the whole thing," Jakes said. "Did you have to grab that stuff?"

"No," Bob admitted. "And if you can't get it free, I'll expect you and Juan to leave me here. It was my own blunder."

Simon had also picked up a couple of rocks and was working, trying to free Bob without touching the stuff. "Aw, come off it. I guess I'd have to see what was underneath, too. Hey, this stuff is really stuck!"

He reached for a knife in the pocket of his suit, but Bob stopped him. "Don't. The stuff doesn't stick to rock, so it must grab metal, like the mitten here. You're going to have to use that knife to cut off my sleeve."

He was already working his arm out of the sleeve of the suit. His eyes swung up toward the empty space above, instinctively looking for alien ships, and his heart was beating more rapidly than it should. But he couldn't let the others see that he was scared.

Jakes caught the sleeve at once, and gave it a quick, tight twist. "Hold it," he told Juan. Then he began sawing at the tough fabric below it. He was sweating, too, and probably as scared as Bob, but his voice was steadier than usual, and his hands didn't shake.

Finally, the sleeve was cut through. There was a slow leak through it, in spite of the twist, but the tank supply made up for that. Jakes yanked out a patch and adhesive, and doubled it over the cut, smearing it with the gooey adhesive. He waited for it to boil dry in the vacuum, and let go of the sleeve.

Probably it leaked a little now, but it would hold. Bob nodded his thanks, and Jakes shrugged, his face flushing. Then they swung about quickly toward the ship. But managing over the ground with one hand held against his side was worse than Bob had thought. He found that it ruined his balance. Simon watched for a second, and then moved to the other side, locking arms with him.

It seemed to take forever to get back to the *Icarius,* and probably did take them several minutes. The grapples on their shoes were already dulling a little, making progress more difficult.

Juan was already in when they reached the ship. Jakes shoved Bob toward the lock, and he didn't argue. By custom, a man with an injury or a defective space suit got all consideration. He moved through the lock as rapidly as he could and began tearing the suit off quickly. A minute later, Jakes came in, already unzipping. He leaped for the pilot's seat, and then stopped.

"Bob, maybe you're right. Maybe we should stop playing a lone hand. Get on the phone and call the Fleet."

"They can't get here any faster than we can get back," Bob pointed out. "While we're sitting here, we could just as well be heading back to Outpost."

Juan shook his head. "No, Bob, I think Simon has himself a point. Look, we are a white ship and we are on white ground here—very hard to see. Also, on all sides are boulders almost as tall as we. In space, we could be found by radar, but here I think we might hide."

"Besides, they probably expect a big Navy tug, and won't even bother looking for us," Jakes added.

In a way, their case made good sense. But Bob shook his head. "Call the Fleet if you want, Simon, but I won't. We got ourselves into it by disobeying orders. Now it's up to us to get out."

"A good old Navy saying, I suppose," Jakes sneered.

"It is," Bob told him. "You can't play both sides of the fence. You either follow the rules or go on your own. But in this case, it's something else. If this trap was set here, it must have been because *they* wanted one of our Navy ships, just as we wanted theirs. We'd be playing right into their hands; even a cruiser would be worth a lot more to them than the *Icarius*. And besides, if the Navy came out for us, how many men would get killed in this trap?"

"You're just scared to stay here. Afraid one of your black ships might come down for you," Jakes told him.

"Sure," Bob admitted. "I'm plenty scared of that. But what are you afraid of—going out where they can see you?"

"Vote," Juan suggested. The others nodded, and he went on. "Thumbs up, we go back. Thumbs down, we stay here."

Bob stuck his thumb up at once, and Simon hesitated. Then his own thumb went up. Juan shrugged and made no attempt to state his wishes. The decision was made and he'd go along with it.

Simon reached for the throttle again, but this time Bob stopped him. "You're half right, though. We should notify the Fleet. If they saw us come here, they may have spotted what we were after and be getting ready to send out tugs, or some sort of ships. We'd better tell them it's a fake, and let them know what they're up against."

Juan nodded quickly at that, and Jakes made no objections, though he obviously didn't like the wasted time, now that they were about to head back. He handed over the microphone to Bob, and set the beam indicator toward Outpost. Bob sent in the standard distress warning signal, together with their identification.

Wallingford's voice answered, cutting through the usual red tape. Obviously, the departure of the *Icarius* had not only been noticed, but had been followed up and brought to the top brass at once. He must have had a line open to Communications every minute.

"All right. Ensign, report."

Bob had begun that as soon as he was acknowledged, since it took several seconds for the signal to travel to Outpost. He summed it up as quickly as possible.

Wallingford's voice came back quickly. "Right. I'm recalling all ships that were headed for your mock-up ship. Consider yourselves under arrest, but get back here as quickly as you can. And good luck!"

Bob cut off, and suddenly noticed that Jakes wasn't there. He turned to see Jakes getting into a suit, fumbling in his effort for haste.

"Darned towrope," Simon said as he fought with the zipper. "Forgot to unhitch it. Without weight at the other end, it'd swing right into the rocks. Might wreck us." He got the zipper closed, and reached for the helmet. "All ships recalled, we're under arrest, and he wishes us good luck! Phooey!"

He was going through the lock a second later. They moved to the viewport to watch him come out and dash for the hitch that held the towline to the ship. Again, his fingers were clumsy with an attempt at speed. He stamped one foot, then had to catch himself quickly as he started to drift upward. Then he stopped, looked up at them, and grinned. Bob knew he was simply trying to force himself to relax. It seemed to work. This time, he unsnapped the line, and sprang back to the lock.

Bob moved forward to help him off with the suit, and they were ready to take off again. But a lot of time had been wasted since they'd discovered the trap. They were a fine bunch of heroes, Bob thought bitterly. They practically needed a nursemaid.

The radar screen snapped on, and Jakes reached for

the throttle. Then he gasped and jerked his hand back. On the screen, three large pips showed up. Straining their eyes, the boys could just make out the black ships that were low on the horizon as the little moon revolved. They hung poised and waiting.

Juan shook his head. "They weren't there before."

"Then maybe they've just arrived," Bob guessed, and hoped he was right. "In that case, if we can just wait without being seen until we're on the other side of the moon, we might get away without being spotted. Besides, we can't take off now. We're pointing away from Outpost. Those ships must be using this moon as a shield to keep them out of the spotting screens at Communications."

The black shapes seemed to rise slowly, higher as the moon rotated, and then to begin sinking. Each second took longer than any second Bob had experienced, and his stomach was sick with the strain of waiting. But he forced himself to seem as cool as he could.

"Nice picture," Simon broke the silence. "We probably get wiped out. If we don't, we go back under arrest."

"What will they do to us, in this being under arrest?" Juan asked.

Bob shook his head. "Nothing much. Don't listen to Simon. When Wallingford told us to consider ourselves under arrest, *but* to get back as soon as we could, he was trying to pass on the word that we didn't have to worry. We broke the rules, but we did keep Navy ships from spotting this and walking into a trap. So we'll probably get a bawling out and be confined to quarters for a while."

Bob hoped he was right, at least. But still he wasn't entirely sure. The warning they'd radioed back would count in their favor, of course. But the Navy during wartime was different from the Navy he knew.

He glanced nervously at the screen, where the ships were almost gone from sight. Apparently they hadn't moved. If the *Icarius* hadn't been spotted, all might yet go off as it should. And it seemed the ships hadn't seen them. The logical time to strike would have been while they were turned away from Outpost.

Now the radar screen began to register the marker pip broadcast from the base. They were swinging around to face Outpost. Jakes fingered the controls nervously, but he knew it was still too soon. He licked his lips, and kept his eyes glued on the screen as the beacon pip crossed it slowly toward the center.

Juan seemed more nervous than Bob or Jakes, but he managed to smile and shrug in a pretense of courage. It was Simon who finally admitted the truth. "I'm scared silly."

"Me too," Bob admitted, glad for the chance to stop pretending. His throat was dry, and his breath ached from holding it in. Then, amazingly, the admission of his fright seemed to make him feel better.

"Dead center," Jakes said suddenly. His fingers bit down on the throttle, and the *Icarius* seemed to jump into the air as if thrown from a catapult.

It was hard to see the screen, but Bob somehow kept his eyes focused on it. It showed nothing but the mark from the beacon. "Better overshoot than reverse too soon," he suggested thickly.

Simon's muffled grunt was mixed with blood roaring in Bob's ears. "Yeah . . . yeah, I figured on that. If we get that far. Maybe we will."

They were half a minute off the moon when the first of the pips hit the screen, just at the edge. Juan cried out at the same time Bob saw them increase from one to three. The black ships were coming out from behind the moonlet, probably deciding to search it thoroughly. Their course didn't look as if they had spotted the little *Icarius,* though that seemed hard to believe.

"Maybe there's time to drop back," he gasped.

Jakes hit the switches, and snapped the *Icarius* over sharply, then cut on the throttle again. But they'd built up enough speed to keep drifting outward for some time before the *Icarius* began moving back toward the moon. There wouldn't be time for them to land where they had been, even if the ships didn't see the small blue flame of their exhaust, or spot them in some electronic device.

Only one thing was left to do, and that was to try to dart around to the side, and somehow get the moon between them again. Jakes was working the controls, his face covered with sweat. This close to a body even the size of the little moon was no place for comfortable navigation, and the three ships on the screen made it a lot harder. He was trying to keep his jets from blasting toward them as much as possible, to increase the chance of not being seen.

Even over the fear that gripped him, Bob felt a sudden thrill of admiration at the way Jakes handled the ship. He'd seen the crack pilots of the Fleet on fancy maneuvers, but he hadn't seen stunting to equal what Jakes was going through. It would be a shame if it was all useless in the end. Shame? It'd be a lot more than that. Bob could remember the way the blue balls of lightning had exploded inside the ships of Wing Nine.

They seemed about to make it, though. The three pips were going down on the screen again, and the *Icarius* was reaching some sort of balance that didn't take constant juggling with the steering jets. If the ships didn't spot them for a few seconds more they might have a chance.

"Find me some kind of rough valley down there," Simon gasped. "Just big enough to bury us in. I'll set her down in anything, if you can spot a good cover."

The little telescreen showed a wild jumble under them, but nothing in which they could hide. Bob seemed to remember one big crevasse visible before they first landed and which would do, but he couldn't spot it.

Then another grunt from Jakes snapped his eyes back to the radar screen. It was too late. The black ships must have spotted them, since they were now heading straight toward the *Icarius*, though without the impossible speeds of which they were capable.

They didn't need to rush. The three inside the little ship were sitting ducks for them.

CHAPTER 11 /

Bound for Planet X

"ONLY ONE CHANCE," Simon gasped. The strain of trying to maneuver under such an acceleration pressure was telling on him. But his hands were still in complete mastery of the controls.

He flipped the ship further over, using the full strength of the steering jets, and went skimming over the little moon, forcing the *Icarius* into a power curve that shot her out of the sight of the three ships. There would, however, be no time for a careful landing before they caught up. Bob couldn't see any chance.

Simon's eyes were glued to the screen, though, and he was cutting almost entirely around the moon. It required a constant turning with the steering rockets to swing the main jet off course enough to keep the circle going.

Ahead of them, the mock-up ship suddenly appeared. Simon headed straight for it. As it came near, he forced the *Icarius* down until she was almost skimming the ground, and began braking furiously. The mock-up swelled in the screen—and behind it lay a mass of ugly boulders. Bob ducked instinctively—or tried to; the pressure in the cushion kept him from doing more than nodding his head.

Something flipped across the observation port. There was a simultaneous blast from the braking rockets, and the *Icarius* gave a screech as her bottom scraped rock. Then she was still.

They were inside the mock-up, placed there almost as if Simon had been a hand and the ship a ball to be dropped into a pocket. Bob sighed, and almost relaxed. It was logical—and the last thing in the world he would have thought of doing. But it was the only really good cover on the whole moon—and perhaps the last place where the aliens would look for them.

Now some of Simon's cockiness came back. "How was that for a landing, boy? Did the Academy make or not make a mistake?"

"Maybe they did," Bob had to admit. "I don't care. What I want to know is how we're going to get out."

"No trouble, I think. That stuff stuck to metal, but it didn't seem to bother anything else. And the *Icarius* has a porcelain glaze all over her. Anyhow, I don't think the stuff is tough enough to worry a set of hydrogen rockets."

Bob shook his head. "I didn't mean that. I mean that we may not be found here, but we still are no nearer getting back to Outpost than before. We can't stay here forever."

"We can stay for a month at least," Simon told him. "I keep her pretty well stocked. Juan, you're pretty good at heating things. Want to fix up a lunch?"

Juan got out of his seat, still looking worried, and began opening lockers and taking out whatever struck his fancy. Most of the cans were of the type which heated the food automatically when a button on top was pressed, and then popped open when it was ready. He selected three of these, and three bulbs of cold tea. Eating here would be easier than in no gravity, but not too much.

The chief trouble with their hide-out, Bob decided, was that they couldn't look out. The blast of the braking rockets had apparently blown the tough fabric up as the ship went through, and it had settled back again. The best plastic fabrics known to men would have been completely consumed, but this stuff seemed to have almost unlimited tolerance to heat, cold, pressure and almost everything else. They were walled in thoroughly.

Reaction set in as he realized they might actually be safe for a while. His hands shook as he took the warm can from Juan, and he noticed that Simon could hardly hold his. But that could be partly sheer physical strain. Operating those controls as he had done against top acceleration pressure must have strained his muscles to the limit.

"They'll hardly hang around a month so near Outpost," Bob decided finally. "If we can stick it out without being found for a few hours, they'll probably go away."

"Yeah." Simon had given up trying to control his muscles. He had found a lever that wasn't present on regulation acceleration chairs and pressed it, to let his seat slope back. Now he half lay on it, sipping at the tea and trying to relax.

"Yeah," he repeated. "If we last a few hours, we'll be all right, I guess. I wish I knew where those aliens are right now."

"You could try the radar," Juan suggested. "It should go through this cloth, should it not?"

"It might. But I don't know whether they can detect it or not. Better leave it off." Simon rolled over and bent his face down, trying to line up the port and his eye in such a way that he could see through the faint slit near the bottom of the mock-up they were in. He gave up.

The inability to see what was going on began to get on their nerves sooner than Bob would have expected. They knew that the black ships were probably somewhere around, and they suspected that the aliens might have ways of detecting them of which they knew nothing. But they couldn't be sure.

Finally, Jakes got up and began straightening up the slight mess their eating had made. Juan started to help, but Simon shook his head. "We'd better stay in our seats. If we have to take off, it'll be pretty sudden."

"You can't take off," Bob told him. "You'd run smack into those boulders ahead."

Jakes frowned and nodded slowly. "Hey, that's right. I forgot all about them. We'd better swing the *Icarius* around, and do it quick. Shouldn't be too heavy here."

That seemed to be the only answer, and they got into their space suits again, which seemed to be a regular job on this moon. Outside, they saw that there was plenty of room for the maneuver under the tent-like dome. And the whole ship shouldn't weigh enough on this moon to bother them.

But the force of inertia was as strong as ever. Here, a man could probably lift a thousand pounds with his little finger. But he couldn't have jerked it up, any more than on Earth. The old law that things resist change of motion with a force proportional to their mass—not merely their weight—still applied. The *Icarius* had a motion of zero, and changing it to anything else took a lot of work and effort. Even with the light weight, there was also some friction working against them—and almost none in their favor to hold them down.

Bob finally solved it by fastening a line to the ship and having the three brace themselves against one of the slim metal supports for the mock-up. It took minutes of straining at the cord to get the ship into a slow motion, barely visible to their eyes, but it did begin turning. And at least there was no sign outside, as there would have been if they'd slewed her around with the steering jets.

Once in motion, it wasn't hard to overcome friction here enough to keep her turning. But at the end, it proved equally hard to stop the ship, and a long process of trial and error was needed to get her lined up to suit Simon Jakes.

This time, they were all sweating from honest labor. Juan started back inside, but Simon and Bob both had the same idea. They flopped down on their stomachs and began peering out under the slit at the bottom of the fabric. When they were close to it—but carefully not touching it—they could see a fair amount of the rocky terrain around them.

Bob slid over beside Jakes and touched helmets with him, not trusting the use of radio, which might carry far enough for the black ships to detect. "We could leave one man outside here to keep guard. And leave the outer seal of the air lock open. Then if things happen, he could make a dash for it, perhaps bang on the inner lock and let the others know it was time to do something. You could take off while I was getting through the inner lock."

"And you could get squashed flat under the acceleration pressure," Simon answered. "Nope. But we might let the air out of the ship, and keep our space suits on. Then we could keep both seals of the lock open."

This seemed like the best idea. Bob ducked his head down and looked out again.

For a second, his heart seemed to explode. Coming down gently as a feather and almost touching the surface was the hull of a great black ship! As he swiveled his gaze, he saw another—and beyond that a third. They were arranged together at the side of the mockup, and there was no question but what they were coming with a full knowledge of where the *Icarius* was hidden!

He touched Jakes and pointed, unable to speak. The older boy glimpsed the ship and jerked. "Back," he said hoarsely. He began scrambling backward over the ground, too startled to think of turning around or getting to his feet. Bob yanked him up, and they scrambled as swiftly as they could toward the lock.

Simon was the logical one to go through first, and he made no protests as Bob gave him a push. The lock moved through its cycle slowly. Then Bob was in it, and finally emerging. Jakes's white face was already free of his helmet. "Strip," he said in a whisper that was as natural as it was ridiculous. "Work the ship better without the suit."

He left the suit lying where it was, Bob following his

example. Now there was no reason for not using the radar. Juan had it turned on, and it showed the three ships among the boulders, mixed with the skeletal framework of the mock-up. Radar never gave a completely clear picture, but something was apparently opening on one of the ships, as if a landing party was in progress.

"Ready," Jakes said. He glanced back, and then set his controls carefully before releasing the lock that kept them inactive.

Bob was getting used to taking off at the full power of the jets. But this had the added flavor of a high scream from the bottom of the ship as it slid over the rough ground, and the view of waiting rocks just ahead, which they barely missed; but the rocks were far behind before this realization struck home. The ship came upward slowly, straightened, and then leaped out into space.

"Where?" Simon asked.

"Outpost," Bob decided instantly. It was the nearest place and the safest. They might have thrown off some pursuit by twisting around and heading down toward Neptune, but that lay millions of miles away, and the aliens obviously had some means of detecting them.

"If they're putting out landing parties, we have some chance," he decided. "It may take a few minutes for them to realize what is going on and get all their men—or whatever they are—back."

Then he saw that his hopes were futile. On the screen, he spotted one of the big ships lifting easily. As he watched, the other two also rose toward them. They were already a fair distance away but that wouldn't mean much if these ships could travel as the other aliens had done.

At first, it didn't seem probable, since they came up from the surface at a leisurely clip, and seemed to be moving about in an aimless fashion. "Looking for us," Jakes guessed. "Either that or making sure we didn't leave someone behind."

It looked more like the latter. The *Icarius* continued to gain distance, while the black ships moved about over the surface, as if directing some type of searching beam downward. Then they all clumped together, and began moving straight upward, toward the *Icarius*.

Jakes groaned and tried to nurse another bit of speed out of his straining jets. But they were already at maximum, and nothing more could be done.

The black ships seemed to be thinking things over for a moment more. Then one of them leaped into an acceleration about twice what the *Icarius* could pull, others seconding the move. The distance began to narrow, more and more rapidly.

They were still less than a fifth of the way to Outpost, and their chances were growing slimmer every second. There was no way to outrun the ships. There was no basis for comparison—it was something like a snail trying to outrun an eagle.

Again the black ships increased their acceleration, until it must have been nearly fifty gravities. Bob hadn't quite believed his memory of the other times, but he believed this. He didn't want to, but there was no way to deny it. The ships were moving toward the *Icarius* at a rate which made the result a matter of a minute or less.

Jakes cut his acceleration. The black ships came up behind and matched course and speed instantly. Two of them spread out, and the third suddenly leaped ahead of the *Icarius* and again matched course. The position of the Planet X ships was an equilateral triangle, with the *Icarius* dead center.

Jakes hit the controls, and shot downward abruptly, curving off to the side as he did so. The other ships were delayed a split second in following him, but a second later they repeated their maneuver of putting him in the center. Then he tried going up. This time the triangle they formed was smaller.

It grew smaller with each maneuver, until the ships were almost touching the *Icarius*. Seen through one of the ports, they were huge, without a sign of a break in their smooth hulls. There were no portholes, though radar had really made these needless for any ships. And there was no evidence of any driving mechanism. They blasted their way through space. Somehow, they simply moved.

The next time Simon tried to move, he found that nothing happened. One of the big ships was touching the *Icarius,* and it seemed to be locking them down, though no mechanical contact of magnetic or hooked grapple had been tried.

The leading ship swung over slowly, until the bottom of one end was in line with the *Icarius*. It began backing up smoothly, while a hatch, twice big enough to engulf the little ship completely, opened in it.

Jakes waited until the sides of the huge opening were at the port, and then cut on his braking rockets. They shot out of the nose of the *Icarius,* with a blast that should have shriveled anything they touched. But nothing happened. The great ship went on backing around them, until they were completely engulfed.

In the viewing screen from the rear, the boys saw the big doors began to shut again. Bob knew now how Jonah had felt when the whale had swallowed him. This looked exactly like such a huge mouth closing down over them.

Then something seemed to suck them sharply downward and they landed with a shrill clang of metal against what was probably the floor of the huge chamber that had swallowed them.

Jakes cut on the lights of the ship trying to make out something of the place where they had been swallowed. But it seemed to be nothing but a room ten times the size of the whole *Icarius*, built of black metal, and without any other features.

The jets of the *Icarius* had obviously been running all along, since Jakes suddenly cut them off. But it made no difference. Then a feeling of weight began to press at their bodies, rising until it had reached about Earth-normal. It stayed there.

"Here we go, bound for Planet X," Jakes muttered. "And right now, since we can't do anything, I'm going to sleep. I'm dead."

He touched the button that turned the seat into a rough couch, and lay back. Bob tried the same, and found it more comfortable than most of the beds in which he had slept. He was surprised to find his own eyes heavy. It didn't seem possible that he could actually fall asleep. But somehow, after the long flight, the fact that there was now nothing at all they could do seemed to leave him dulled and drowsy.

His last thought was a sudden wonder about what would happen to them if the alien ship ever tried jumping up to her top gravity of acceleration. But there was nothing he could do about that either!

CHAPTER 12 /

A Matter of Language

WHEN THEY AWOKE, there was the same feeling of normal gravity as before. Bob got up groggily and located material for a simple breakfast. He had no way of knowing what time it was, but he suspected that the long chase had taken more hours than they had realized. That would account for some of their sleepiness.

Juan was studying the blackness of the chamber in front of their ship. He took the food from Bob, and began eating listlessly, his eyes still fixed outward. "I have a theory," he announced.

He dug into the food, then swallowed thoughtfully. "I think that what we feel here is not the pressure of acceleration at all. It doesn't change, and it is much too slow for the ship's, if what we have seen is true. What we feel is real gravity—a gravity made right in these ships. Consider. If they can control gravity, then they are indeed advanced, wouldn't you say?"

"We know that already," Bob answered. "But you may be right about the gravity here. I wonder if they move the same way—control gravity and make it pull them toward or away from whatever they like?"

"I have considered that, too," Juan put in. Then he shook his head. "But it is not so logical. If they can control gravity, they may control inertia. They may be able to say to inertia, go away—and it will go away for them. Then with the slightest effort, they can reach any speed; the mass of this ship will not object to changing its speed, it will take no work to change it. And because we inside also have no inertia for that change of speed, we do not even feel it. It is as if there had been no change, even though we leap from no speed forward to millions of miles an hour. That way, they can stop dead after any speed and not be hurt."

It was a good enough theory, though a surprising one. There had been a little theoretical work done which indicated that inertia was not a fixed thing, but nobody had been able to prove it. Still, if the ship could repeal inertia whenever it wanted to, it would explain things fairly well.

"Then where are we now?" Simon asked. His face was dulled with sleep, but seemed somehow less stupid than it had been. Maybe he was developing.

"We are on Planet X, of course," Juan announced. "We have slept for many hours, and they can travel at any speed. So we have arrived."

That wasn't just a theory, they found a few minutes later. The great door at the rear snapped open to show what might almost have been a country meadow back on Earth. Grass grew lushly and there were trees everywhere. Above, the sky was filled with soft clouds. But none of the trees looked exactly like normal Earth ones. There was a subtle difference about everything.

Something similar to a car, but on three wheels, came rolling up a ramp, and stopped beside the lock of the *Icarius*. There was the sound of the outer lock opening. Bob jumped to the viewing port, but he could see nothing of the occupants of the car.

"Hey, suppose they're cannibals!" Jakes breathed.

It was nothing to the thoughts that were churning in Bob's mind. He really hadn't tried to picture the aliens before, but now every fantasy he had read seemed to come to his mind. Walking plants, lizards with giant heads, things with arms like octopuses, and a horde of monsters of every shape. He drew his knife slowly, opening the big blade.

The inner lock opened cautiously. It was darker than

the inside of the *Icarius,* and Bob could make out only a vague shape. Then the creature stepped forward.

The shock was worse than any monster could have given them. The alien from Planet X looked almost exactly like a human!

He was a short man, and his knee joints looked a little wrong; there wasn't the usual knobbiness. The hand that held some kind of a weapon had four normal fingers, but there was a thumb opposite the regular one, giving him a double palm. Yet even the fingernails were there. Generally, his body seemed almost completely normal. His ears were a bit too large, and there was no hair on his head, while his eyes had a vaguely Asiatic slant to them. His skin was an orange shade, not too different from some jaundiced people, but still unmatchable on Earth.

Yet even on Earth, he would hardly have attracted a second glance. He was dressed in something like a Scotch ceremonial kilt of solid blue, with a soft T shirt and a brief cape. On a wide belt at his waist, several pouches were sewn. The costume was no odder than the man.

He stepped further into the *Icarius,* his eyes resting in amusement on the knives that Jakes and Bob held. He tapped his pistol-like weapon confidently, and made a motion of throwing something away, pointing at the knives. The two boys took the hint, and he smiled pleasantly at them.

"Vla no yoga," he told them in a soft, educated voice. *"Nikomi ol Thule. Vu yara ultai san vorstala?"*

"Sounds like he's telling us hello and welcome to this world," Bob guessed. He saw Juan blink his eyes in surprise—probably a delayed reaction at the fact an alien spoke what might almost have been a human language. "Wonder what his question was?"

"Aw, probably wants us to take a ride in his buggy," Simon answered. "And from the motions he's going through, that's no guess."

There were two other creatures waiting outside as the

boys emerged. They looked much like the first, except for minor details. At the sight of the three humans, they both smiled, and moved to open the door of the three-wheeled car. Even that was surprisingly human—or not so surprising, since both races would obviously have the same ideas of comfort. It was a large vehicle, with room for the three humans in back and jump seats where the two guards could ride facing them. The first alien climbed behind the rod that served as a wheel and backed the little distance down the ramp. Then he swung the car around, and began heading for a city some distance away.

Bob sat next to a window, and his eyes were busy. He might be killed the next minute—after all, smiles might not mean kindness here—but at least he'd get an eyeful.

The overall picture was still Earthlike, though thousands of details of leaves and roads and birds were different. They were apparently in a sort of combination park and spaceport—which was logical enough, where spaceships needed no rocket blast, and where heavily loaded vehicles probably nullified part of the gravity acting on them. Bob noticed that there was very little room in the car for an engine, and that it ran smoothly and quietly. They were following a well-used road along part of the park now, where other ships lay spread about casually.

Then they turned and headed for the city proper. Again, the sights were not too startling. In many ways, the architecture looked more open and rounded than on Earth; there were few square corners, and more doors and windows. The tallest building was only eight stories high, but many were wider than any usual buildings on Earth. This must have been the business section, but there were little parks everywhere. Beyond, he caught a glimpse of what might be a suburb, with many small buildings spread about in a rambling fashion. The major difference from Earth was a feeling of greater comfort and an absence of bright signs and loaded shop windows.

Now they drove up to the tallest building, and the three guards walked behind, pointing out the way up an escalator to the top floor. He then turned to a moving belt which carried them down a large open hall toward a wide door at the end. They stepped off, and were obviously facing someone of authority. The man there on the platform, containing a table and a comfortable chair, was older than the others and he radiated power of some sort.

Now Bob spotted others in the huge room. One wall was covered with machinery that might have been calculators and electronic brains. Another was composed of wide windows looking out on a park. And scattered about casually were a large number of chairs. The guards motioned the three boys into comfortable ones near the banks of machines.

It all seemed so relaxed and friendly that Bob's guard had been going steadily down. He dropped into the chair without a second thought, and the other two did the same.

Beside him, a man suddenly dropped a huge mechanical gadget over his head and locked it on deftly with a single motion. Bob heard Jakes's frenzied yell, and saw that Simon and Juan were receiving the same treatment.

It had been smart to lull him first, and then spring torture on him suddenly. But it wouldn't work. He gritted his teeth as another older man came out and was fitted with a different type of machine, one that trailed long wires after it, and completely covered his neck and the back of his head. He wasn't going to give away any of the Federation secrets, no matter how much they tortured him.

The man in front of them began reading from a book in a soft voice, going slowly. Something tingled in Bob's mind. He struggled to resist it. So it wouldn't be torture, but hypnotism. Well, he'd had a few courses in how to resist that, too.

The tingling still went on, though. And suddenly the words began to sound less strange, and to take on meaning. It was a repetitious thing, with a slow shift through new words to still newer ones. But he found them sinking in, and no longer foreign. It was perfectly natural that a "Nota should Glur"—just as natural as that a Man should Sleep.

There must have been some hypnotic quality to the process, because he suddenly awakened to find that the machine was gone from his head. He stood up and looked around to see the helmets all being packed away. Then a brisk knock from the platform caught his attention and he turned to face the older man there.

"You are, of course, on the planet Thule," the man said quietly, using the Thulian language which now seemed as normal to Bob as English. "As you see, we've taught you our language. Believe me, we're as surprised as you are to find our two races so much alike, not only physically but mentally. It is a mystery. We have no way of knowing whether all races evolve as we two have done on worlds like this, or whether it is a great coincidence. We are not alike in all ways of course. You have one heart and we have two. You have thirty-two teeth, and we have six less. And so on. But let us begin by admitting that we are all human beings. You are our captives, but you are *not* captives of alien monsters. So don't strain yourselves looking for motives that wouldn't be normal if you had been captured by opposing groups on your own planets."

He paused, then smiled at them. "Frankly, we're very happy to have you to study, because we can probably learn more from you than from older people. You're too valuable to us for us to mistreat, because we hope to learn to get along with your people through you. You'll be studied of course. But you have complete freedom of this city, and you'll be given homes, just like anyone else. We want to observe you in real life, not in false surroundings. And now, welcome to Thule. I'm the president of this world—Orsa Faskin. Your names?"

They gave them, half-convinced of the sincerity of the man. Faskin nodded, and introduced them to their guards, using only first names. Ondu, the first one aboard the ship, Wilna and Valin. Then, apparently satisfied, Orsa turned back to other work. The guards had put their weapons away and now came forward.

"We'll be living next door to you, wherever you are. A choice partly up to you," Valin told them. "But since you have no women with you, you might find our hotel comfortable. It's right in this building, underground for silence, of course."

"Who cares where we go?" Simon asked. "Sure, put us up in this fancy jail of yours."

"It's no jail. You'll have the same privileges as any citizen of Thule, or as nearly so much as we can possibly arrange."

"Suppose we try to escape?" Bob asked quickly.

Valin looked surprised. "Where? You could leave the city probably—though we'd rather you didn't without consulting us first. But this whole planet is your jail—you can't escape."

"You've got spaceships," Bob persisted.

"Certainly. But it takes at least twenty people to work one of our ships—we have no small ones. Even if you learned how, you couldn't use them. And you couldn't force twenty men, scattered over a huge ship, by threatening them with weapons. As for your own charming ship—that will be securely locked down in a public square for the people of Thule to see."

Simon looked completely unconvinced. "And I suppose we can buy weapons?"

"No, because we don't use money yet," Valin told him. "But you can have my weapon now if it will make you feel better. Since you're a civilized man, I feel quite safe. You wouldn't use it against me unless you could gain by it. There is nothing to gain. If you need anything, ask for it and you'll have it—except a chance to leave Thule."

Bob reached out a hand as Jakes shook his head. "I'd

like that, Valin," he said. He took the weapon and turned it over, trying to see how it worked. There was a tiny trigger, and a rifled barrel, but he couldn't see the works.

"Compressed gas," Valin said. "The bullet is made of wax containing a drug that spreads through the skin and paralyzes. It also leaves a nasty bruise. Here, you'll find gas capsules and bullets in this. It's as effective as the explosives and lead guns we previously used, and a lot less messy."

They were riding down the escalator now, and switched to another that went down about eight stories below the ground. Bob saw that much of the traffic here was underground, and they had subways, with cars riding on a single rail. Then they came to the "lobby" of the "hotel," where Valin asked for two suites—one for his party and one for Bob's. There was considerable consultation before they decided on a setup which would be generally satisfactory.

The boys' suite turned out to be rather simply furnished, but comfortable by any standards, including a little communication unit that led to the food-supply department, and a small elevator to bring their orders up. But there were no bellboys, and he found that they would have to clean their own place. Valin seemed surprised at the idea of men who served others directly.

Juan stretched out on the bed, considering things. "It is nice here, Bob," he decided. "I think I like these people. It is a shame we must kill them or have them kill us."

"You mean you believe all that guff?" Jakes asked incredulously. "You think they're all sweetness and light, like they pretend? Juan, you need more stuff in your head than that think-tank of theirs can put in it."

"But a whole world isn't a lie," Juan objected.

"No—and this isn't a whole world. Look, they get themselves three kids—nice and young, easy to handle; you heard the way the old goat put it. Three kids who come from a military base and know how to run spaceships. They can beat us up, and probably get nothing. Or they can slick up part of a city, and soften us up until we spill everything they might want to know." Simon spread his hands. "Those guys have to find out plenty about the Solar System—and we're elected prize suckers to tell them."

Bob nodded unhappily. The trouble was that it was going to be hard to resist them. They were probably very good at taming wild beasts—and savage men like the three of them!

CHAPTER 13 /

The World of Thule

VALIN ASSURED BOB that they did indeed have a library, that the language course had included reading, and that there were such things as newspapers to be had in the library. He tagged along on the excuse of showing Bob the way, and then quietly disappeared with a book of his own, leaving the Federation captive surrounded by several books and a pile of the pamphlets which served as newspapers.

Bob had selected the books himself. He was sure that the people of Thule might want to fool him, but equally sure that the whole city wasn't a hoax. That meant that the library was genuine. Books for a people's own use might have some propaganda in them, but they'd be altogether more honest than anything he would get by asking questions.

He sat studying through their histories and recent Thule happenings for the rest of the day, except once when Valin had wandered in to suggest that they eat. The food at the nearest food department wasn't anything Bob could rave about, but he found it edible, and there were a couple of things he even liked. Then he went back to his reading. By the time the library closed and Valin guided him back to the hotel, he had a fair idea of what Thule was all about.

Thule had originally been a planet around another star, almost eighty light-years away. It had had a climate similar to that of Earth; the sun had been bigger and hotter, but the distance to Thule had been greater, to make up for it. Life there had pursued a pattern similar to that on Earth, beginning some billions of years ago and evolving through all its various forms until there were men.

And again, history had been similar. Egypt and Rome had their types, though never quite the same. Actually, the difference began in what might be called the Rome of their history. Instead of declining into an empire, it had split into two separate republics, one of which had been forced to compete against the other with smaller manpower and less resources. The competition had gotten science started far in advance of Earth's history, and at a more rapid pace.

A thousand years after the first split, the two republics had again been united into one, this time over the whole world. Ships fled from planet to planet—and their sun had nearly five times as many planets as the sun of Earth.

Then disaster had come. Another star was moving toward their sun. The two would come close—so close that both would erupt toward each other, filling the space with flaming magma, and both probably going through a stage where they blew up completely shortly after separation. Such "novas" occurred regularly, but knowing that it was normal didn't help them to bear it. In the nova stage, a sun would spread out until it covered nearly all of its planets, before gradually sinking back to its normal size.

All life was sure to be destroyed. At first, they tried the idea of building great spaceships to try to reach planets around another star. But rocket power simply wasn't enough to accomplish this in any livable time; then, too, only a few could go. They began searching for other means than rockets for moving things.

Here Bob had done a double-take, since it had come so close to fitting with Juan's theories. Juan had been close, though wrong in some respects.

They had finally discovered that inertia was not an absolutely inevitable property of matter. It had something to do with the outer shell of electrons and other particles—shell, Bob thought, trying to translate it; it didn't make much sense, since he had always considered such particles to be single things, not the complicated things the Thulians considered them. But the word was as close as he could get to a translation.

They had found that inertia could be adjusted. It could be made "thinner" in one direction than in others. This had meant that once beyond the field of strong gravity, even a gentle thrust might drive them at incredible rates. Normally in space, a man who weighed two hundred pounds and threw a two-pound weight away from him at one hundred feet a minute would drift back one foot per minute himself. But when inertia was made "thin" in the direction of the man's drifting, the same weight at the same speed might make him drive along at a speed of anything from one to one hundred thousand times that of the weight!

They had long explanations as to why this didn't violate the conservation of energy, but Bob skipped those. The result, anyhow, was that they could erect ships now of any size to travel at nearly any speed and distance. And having this discovery, they realized that their whole world could be a spaceship.

There had been many problems to solve first, of course. They had been forced to find some way of keeping the planet warm and lighted while away from the sun. This had come through some obscure work on light done years before, with the result that energy could be released directly into the air. Bob had noticed that there were no shadows on Thule. Now he understood. Each atom of the atmosphere contributed to the light, instead of it coming from above. Heat was generated in the same way.

It had taken them over a century to get ready, and they had developed other new devices, such as the method of using their energy directly against space, and not needing even tiny rockets. Then the invading star had been near, and they had sailed out beyond the widest limit of danger. They had watched the stars come together, and had seen their own explode outward afterward. They had also watched it shrink back. But instead of returning to normal, it had become shrunken and cold, almost useless to them.

There had been despair at first, and then high courage. With full knowledge that they could not find enough sources of energy to make the whole trip, they had still plotted a course that would lead them to Earth's sun, which they considered most suitable. And they had begun their great journey across nearly five hundred million million miles.

Before their energy began to run low, another discovery was made. One of their greatest scientists learned how to freeze and re-warm the tissues of bodies so rapidly that it would not harm them; the crystals had no time to form in the blood. And at nearly absolute zero, life would lie dormant. It could be wakened a thousand or a million years later without even realizing that time had passed.

All but a few of the inhabitants had the treatment and were carefully stored away in great underground vaults. Then the last few reversed the apparatus that put energy into the air. In a few brief minutes, the whole planet was covered with solid oxygen and all life other than human had been frozen as quickly as the men and women so carefully stored.

With their duty done, the last few were treated in automatic machines, and the planet drifted on through space without life. For nearly two thousand years it sailed on, drawing slowly nearer to the sun. And at last, when it was ten thousand million miles away, automatic alarms were tripped. The same men who had put the world to sleep were now revived. The energy that had been sucked from the atmosphere was restored just as quickly. In an hour, the grass was growing as if nothing had happened, and birds were singing in the trees. And still far away, but already bright in the sky, lay the new sun that was to be their home.

It was then that they had discovered that the sun already had planets. This was small cause for worry, of course. But the discovery that the planets were inhabited by creatures of intelligence had come as a profound shock. It had meant the possibility that their right to a new home would be contested.

A ship had explored the new planet body quickly, and had returned with the report that the men there were even like the Thulians—and that the race was younger and more savage, but well along the road toward a technology that would soon be unconquerable.

By now, Bob was in the periodicals. Here he found a long debate on what should be done. Thule could go on toward other stars, of course—but her energy supplies were running low, and pulling a world away from the gravity of a sun, even by using gravity deflecting means, which weren't too efficient—took energy in great amounts.

They had determined that they must try to settle here, either in peace or by conquest. That had never been fully determined. Some felt that any peace was better than war, but most seemed to doubt that real peace was possible with the men of this sun, and that they would have to conquer first, and try to find peace later.

Then had come the question of reviving all the sleepers, and that was another matter which was postponed, rather than settled. Generally, they seemed to hope that they would not have to revive the others until they were sure it was possible to live here. There seemed to be some vague danger of mental shock to too many wakenings, readjustments, and sleepings again.

As a compromise, they had wakened only five million people out of the five billion population. With these, as they now saw it, it should be possible to settle the issue, one way or another.

Their reactions to the recent trouble were more interesting to Bob than anything else—and harder to figure out. Like men on Earth, they had a bad habit of taking it for granted that words could mean things they didn't mean at all. To Earth, for instance, the word colony had long meant inferiority; and even today, to the Federation, alien meant something dangerous. The Thulians had their own tricks.

They talked about peace, and attack, and all the other things in ways which showed that they meant more than just the words. Until Bob could get to know them fully, he wouldn't be able to be sure of anything.

One thing was certain. The "attack" on Thule by the forces of Wing Nine had come as a profound shock. In their accounts, they had seen military ships arriving, without any accompanying ship which would carry an ambassador or other civilian who could speak for peace. Apparently, then, on Thule a military man dealt only in fighting, and peace was discussed by other groups, who did not have anything to do with military affairs. This might even have its advantages, Bob thought, but they took it for granted that peace was peace and war was war. This led to some strange results when applied to the Navy, whose biggest job was being ready for war in the hope of making permanent peace.

They had hoped that it was only a token force, since it was small, and that it was merely a group coming out to challenge them. (The act of challenge was a formal thing here, and anyone had a right to turn it down. Without it, fighting was considered something too horrible to indulge in.)

They had sent out a larger force, to show that they appreciated the courtesy. But they had then sent what would seem to be an obvious signal not to accept the challenge, and that they did not want to fight. This had been overlooked. Finally, their commander had gently picked up the Federation ships and turned them around, even giving them a good send-off of speed toward their own base. This was intended to show that they really meant not to accept the challenge, as well as to indicate that they bore no hard feelings toward the Federation.

Then right in the midst of this act of courtesy, the Federation ships had opened fire—and with weapons so terrible that they had long been outlawed on Thule—weapons which were dangerous to use, and to manufacture, since a few of them could ruin a whole planet. It had been a sneaking act, an act of pure treachery.

Thule had defended herself, as had been necessary. But when the Federation forces turned to flee, she had not followed them to demand that they be captives, as she had a right to do. Instead, she had let them go back unharmed. That should have convinced them that she had no desire to fight, and that they should send no more forces until she could make up her mind what to do about the Federation.

But now ships were assembling on a moon of Neptune to attack Thule probably. After the challenge had been repeatedly refused, these strange humans were going ahead with a war anyhow. It was unthinkable.

And it seemed to prove once and for all that these humans could never be trusted. They were still savages at heart. The only safe thing to do, according to the views of the periodical, was to use their own weapons—to make the outlawed lithium bombs and to carry enough to all the planets to kill off life there. It would take years before the planets could be used by Thule, of course, but this was the only reasonable action.

Other writers differed, but there was no way of knowing which represented the majority. Bob saw only that all of them were shaken by what his father had tried as a method of finding peace and which they were completely convinced was an act of war, and it looked as if those who favored extermination of the human race might win the debate.

He wondered how a human account of the engage-

ment would sound to a Thulian. On the way back, he
tried to explain to Valin what had really happened.

The man listened politely. At the end he nodded
thoughtfully. "I am glad all your people are not so dis-
courteous, Bob. Your father sounds rather barbarous,
but like an ethical man. Still . . . you admit your lead-
ers cannot control your underleaders. Your father could
not keep this captain from firing? Yes. And you admit
that your people decided on war *before* they listened to
his account in the first place? And you also admit that
your race uses the *same* men to make peace as to start a
war—which means that you do not really separate
peace and war, but get them all confused?"

He shook his head sadly. "I'll have to think this over.
I have always hoped that we could learn to live with
your people, Bob. But after your account, I wonder if
they can accept peace with us, or whether we dare let
them go on beside us."

He turned into his own suite, still puzzled.

Bob had the answer as to how one Thulian, at least,
reacted to man.

And the trouble was that he couldn't be sure that
Valin wasn't right. He'd seen that Thule had many confused ideas, and a mixture of strange sense and tradi-
tional nonsense. If they couldn't help it, how could he
help having false values of his own. Maybe clear logic
would place the same interpretation on events as Valin
had placed on them.

He suspected that the truth was somewhere in between, or that both were wrong. But this didn't help
any. Certainly he couldn't go around explaining things
to everyone here—it would only lead to more trouble.

As far as he could see, neither side wanted war. And
yet both sides were being driven closer and closer to
what they didn't want. Each felt that the other was too
dangerous for them to share a sun with.

And the way it was working out, both were right.

He remembered the idea of sending lithium bombs
against the planets. With their ships, they might suc-

ceed; but not before some of the Federation forces had managed to send suicide squads in on Thule with the same medicine.

It might wind up with the sun having ten planets instead of nine, and no living intelligence on any of them!

CHAPTER 14 /

In Silken Chains

JUAN SEEMED TO LOSE INTEREST after the first day, which was no particular surprise to Bob. The boy had been pushed from pillar to post, from his own world into life on a freighter, then in tragedy to the inner circle of a military machine. He'd been tossed back to the outskirts of that machine, and had gone to work, only to go out on a mad chase. Now he was in still another life. This one, at least, had some advantages for him. He was no more a stranger than Simon or Bob, and life here was a comfortable one, even a pleasant one.

Most of his time seemed to be spent in seeing the pre-migration films made by Thule—outright romance and adventure stories which were always given a touch of fantasy by the difference in the Thule point of view. There were millions of such films in the near-by vault, and Juan seemed to go no further. He did take care of the suite for them, however, and neither Bob nor Simon had any objections to that.

Simon and Bob roamed around, sometimes together and sometimes alone. On the surface, they had complete freedom. Nobody stopped them from anything, except that they were barred from one building. It had something to do with high scientific policy, but it seemed to be more a matter of safety, as Valin said, than of secrecy. The Thulians themselves were barred from the building, unless they had special reasons for being there.

Nobody tried to keep them from examining anything they wanted. And most of the citizens were apparently eager to explain anything they didn't understand.

On the theory that this city might be specially selected for them, Bob asked permission to fly halfway around their world and visit another. Valin spent several hours arranging for special transportation, but there was no objection at any point. They were flown in a stratosphere rocket, making the trip with no one else on board, and Bob found the second city to be no different from the first, except that it was smaller and even more sparsely inhabited. With ninety-nine per cent of the population still in suspended animation, it wasn't too surprising that the world seemed rather empty, and that most of the factory cities were entirely shut down.

Yet there were always the guards. Wherever Bob went, he found Valin tagging along, always with a legitimate excuse. Jakes was having the same trouble with Ondu. Bob came back from his flying visit to find Jakes stamping around, demanding to be let alone, or at least given someone younger. That seemed like a safe request, since neither one of the boys had met anyone who wasn't at least thirty. The young men were still in suspended animation, it seemed.

Ondu shrugged mildly. "I'm only trying to help you, Simon. This is a big world, and a new one. You might get lost or in trouble. I'm responsible for your safety." He reflected then, hands outspread. "But if you're tired of me, we'll have to find someone else. Someone younger, you want?"

"That's right. Someone younger—plenty younger!" Simon told him.

His request was granted the next day. Ondu came in with a boy of about thirteen, who seemed both afraid and eager to meet the men from the Federation. "This is Emo, our president's son," he told Simon. "He is the only young one we have revived."

Bob grinned, in spite of himself. The Thulians always

managed to find some way, it seemed—even if they had to enlist their president's family. He waited for Jakes to blow up at having a boy that much younger.

But Simon only grinned, and held out his hand after a second's thought. "That's fine, Ondu. Couldn't be better. Hi, Emo, I hope you won't mind wasting time on someone who needs a little help?"

Emo broke out in a toothy smile, and they went off together, while Juan and Bob stared at each other, trying to figure Jakes out.

News came through from Outpost, finally. A Thulian ship had made a quick night trip—technically night for Outpost, since it was when most of the officers slept. With the aid of high-speed photography, they had come back with some information. Bob and the others were furnished with copies of it at once, but there was nothing very impressive there. From the photographs and groupings of the ships, it looked as if Outpost was about halfway along with its preparations to invade Thule. But none of them were trained to interpret such matters.

"We dropped a picture of you three to show that you were well, and also that letter you wrote your father," Valin told Bob casually.

Bob puzzled over it, until he remembered the note he had written one night when he was bothered with loneliness. He'd put a lot of information in it about Thule, and only a few personal things, because he'd only written it to kill time. He'd been sure that it would never reach his father. Valin had asked about it once when he saw it, Bob had answered truthfully, and that was the end as far as he was concerned. Now he wished he'd written more, both personal and informative.

"Too bad he can't answer," he told Valin.

The guide looked surprised. "Why not? Naturally, we would permit a single ship to fly over and drop anything smaller than a bomb. One can't break up families, unless communication is impossible."

Bob had never quite gotten the family relationships clear here, but he gathered that they were a good deal closer than on Earth, and that they also involved some degree of politics. The president was a part of every family, as were his wife and children.

But he knew that no Federation ship would fly over. It would seem like simple suicide.

It was after that that Valin suggested he might call Outpost on the radio. The permission carried certain obligations, however. He would be required to read a prepared paper to the Naval heads at Outpost, giving the opinions of Thule. The translation would be up to Bob.

He almost agreed, but decided to consult with Jakes. And Jakes couldn't see it. "Sure, act as propaganda bureau."

"What difference does it make, if it helps bring the two sides together in any way?" Bob wanted to know.

Jakes was suddenly serious. "Bob, are you falling for these people. Are you beginning to believe them?"

"I like them," Bob had to admit. "There's a lot of good in Thule."

"Sure there is. And there's a lot of good in the Federation. Hey, look. They want you to like them. That's probably the whole idea of our being here. You get to like them, and they have you call up Outpost and tell them things you think are true. They want to make a traitor out of you, Bob. And I'm not going to stand for that."

He was pacing up and down the room, his scraggly blond hair bouncing up and down on his forehead, and making him look completely ridiculous. But for once, he didn't sound ridiculous.

"Suppose we had young Emo on Outpost," he went on. "We'd fix him up, keep him amused, give him all the candy he wanted. And we'd have him call Thule. Oh, we'd give him the truth to speak. How we didn't want war, everything your father believes. Right? And you know what we might do then? When he got them about softened up and believing us, the side that thinks we have to have war would hop right in and knock Thule for a cocked hat. Look at your history. It's full of such acts."

Bob thought the matter over slowly, and finally was forced to agree. What they would give him to say might very well be true, but it would be one side of the truth, and not the side having the most power.

"All right," he agreed, "I'll wait until I know more about it. Maybe I am a little naïve right now."

"You were just about being made a sucker of," Jakes told him firmly.

He went over to the door and locked it firmly. When he came back, he wore the air of a trained conspirator—trained in some movie lot, that is. His voice was barely a whisper. "Wait a minute."

Some of his things had been transferred from the *Icarius,* and one of the objects was a leather brief case with a combination lock. He went to it now and unlocked it, dragging out a sheaf of papers. He selected two of them and spread them out carefully.

"There," he announced proudly, "is what I've been doing. The plans of most of their weapons. Here's that ball-lightning thing. And here's their pressor-ray gadget. I don't know just how they work, but I can read enough to give any real scientist all he needs. How's that for being a spy?"

"Where were they?"

"In that science building they kept us out of." Jakes chuckled. "Why do you think I took young Emo as my guide? Not for fun, I can tell you. He's a good kid, but he keeps asking so many questions about the Federation my tongue gets tired before luncheon. But *he* can get into that building. And when he wants to go in, he takes anyone else in with him. Big guided tour, with half a dozen men to make sure he doesn't get in any trouble. They were so busy watching him I spent half an hour alone back in the files!"

Bob tried to believe it had been that simple. It was

true that the family relationships here, plus the fact that Emo was technically a son of every man on the planet, would make for a lot of attention. But if Jakes had been shown the files and left alone with them, there must have been good reasons for it.

"I've plans for getting out of here," Jakes told him. "I haven't got them entirely worked out, but there's one way, and I intend to be ready for it. When I go, these go with me. There's everything here. How that inertia gadget works, how they feed power into the air, artificial gravity, everything. I went through the whole list and skimmed the best of it."

"And I suppose you walked right out with them, and they offered to gift wrap them at the door?"

Jakes snorted. "Go on, be funny. I was carrying this brief case with me at the time. I had it full of stuff I took out of the library, so I just chucked these in with them. Nobody even asked to see them."

"It's still too easy. If these plans are really worthwhile, they wouldn't make it that simple." Bob was getting more worried as he thought about it.

"It's always easy if it works," Jakes told him. "That's what spies count on, I'll bet. A lot of luck, like young Emo figuring Federation men are the same as we used to think cowboys and Indians were, and being the president's son. And a little bit of pure nerve. Maybe I don't always think my father's wonderful, but he's got nerve. I guess I take after him."

He put the papers back carefully, and shoved the brief case into a closet. "How about going to look at the old *Icarius?* I heard they had her on exhibition at Center Park. And that her galley is still stocked with decent food."

Bob had been about to turn it down, but the mention of food decided him. He thought about calling Juan, but then gave up the idea. Juan claimed he was learning more about the people of Thule from the old films than they could discover in ten years of living with them.

He'd objected once when Bob had tried to get him to skip his studies for a day. Let him sit in the vault if he wanted to. Besides, they could always bring back some of the food for him.

Valin and Emo appeared in the door as if by accident as they were leaving and dropped in beside them. Emo led them proudly to a subway that took them directly to Center Park.

The *Icarius* was the center of attention there, though few people seemed to want to go inside through the lock. On Earth or Mars, everything movable would have been stripped clean by curious collectors, but here all was exactly as it had been left.

Valin explained the way it was fastened down, with nothing showing on the surface; it simply seemed to be sitting on its tail fins, poised for an immediate take-off. But ten feet away in a circle, there were small devices buried in the ground. They held the *Icarius* in as firm a net as iron bars could have done, safe from wind, hurricane—or theft by Federation men who wanted to go home. It was the only example of the possibility of tractor rays Bob had seen, and he was surprised when he walked through one of the beams and felt nothing. They could be set for an exact distance, it seemed, and nothing between mattered.

The trip turned out to be a flop, as far as Bob was concerned. The food was good, but he had too many other things on his mind, including the stolen papers. Even Emo's serious attempts to like Mulligan stew didn't impress him.

He was glad when Jakes finally cleaned up and went into the small closet to wash up, and followed him in, just as the older boy let out a yell.

The light there had burned out, and Jakes was staring at his hands in the semidarkness. They were glowing a pale green.

Bob shut the door with a snap, squeezing in with his mouth against Simon's ear. "Hide them!" he whispered.

"I told you it was too easy. Those papers have fluorescent ink on them—and you must have left a fine trail, if they ever look for them."

Maybe it wouldn't matter too much. And maybe Jakes had doomed all three of them by his easily traceable theft!

CHAPTER 15 /

Message from Outpost

THE COCKINESS WAS GONE from Jakes by the time they reached their suite again. Juan looked up from a Thulian book and started to grin. Then his face sobered as he saw them. "What goes on?" he asked in Thulian.

Bob told him as quickly as he could, and the boy began to echo their worry at once. Even if they had been citizens of Thule, such a theft could result in a death sentence, or whatever Thule used to punish its traitors and spies. As it was, there was no way of guessing what might be done to them.

Jakes was washing his hands. They managed to unscrew the cold-light bulb in the bathroom first, so that he could check himself as he scrubbed. The other lights all worked on switches. With them off, there were only a few spots that showed any of the green, and they came off with strong applications of detergent. But the brief case was loaded with it on the outside. Juan fell to, while Jakes took care of all his clothes.

The job was finally finished, but Bob was still shuddering over what might have happened if Valin had come in when the room was dark.

"It still doesn't take care of the marks you probably left all over the files," Bob reminded Jakes. "Successful spies! One of the simplest things to look for."

"Sure, I know. I've seen thrillers, too, and it's in all of them. But how was I to know that the same techniques would apply here? Anyhow, some marks must be

137

left over from a good long time before, because the old guy who showed us around opened 'em up—and his prints would be all over, too."

Jakes was still convinced that he'd gotten away with it, even after Bob argued with him half of the night. Bob guessed he was arguing partly in the hopes that he too could be convinced Jakes was right. But he still had a feeling inside him that Thule knew what had happened, and was only playing cat-and-mouse with them.

He knew what would be true in his own culture's security blanket. And Thule was as busy preparing for war in its own way as the Federation was. They had installed a ring of alarms at a distance of a hundred thousand miles outside the planet, and there were automatic missiles waiting below to take off on the inertia-free drive at whatever sector was touched. They hoped that it was safe enough to prevent any penetration, even by guided bombs. But they weren't sure.

In such an atmosphere, their security blanket was apt to be as tight as that of the Federation.

Finally Jakes managed to change the subject. "Study those locks on the *Icarius?*" he asked. "They're neat, eh? But not as smart as Thule thinks, because they look just like one of the gadgets in the plans; I figured they might use something like that. And when the time comes and some other things work out, I can release them in almost no time. Then maybe you'll be glad I got the plans that will give the Federation everything Thule's got."

Bob turned over and tried to go to sleep, but the last words rankled. He wouldn't be glad of it, he knew. It might be the right thing to take the plans back, if they could get away with it. It was what the Federation would want. But it would destroy the last faint hope of ending the war.

Even now, there was some chance. Thule seemed to be more slanted toward holding off until she could reach Earth's orbit and make a careful study of the people in general than of going to war now. And while the

Federation was planning for war, the papers he had seen at Outpost had shown how sickening the idea was to them. With a little time, something might be worked out.

Not, however, after those plans reached Outpost. With them, Earth and Mars would know that Thule was not merely filled with clever weapons, but that she was scientifically centuries ahead. She would be too far advanced to risk as a neighbor. This was not only true in war—but also held good in shipping, manufacturing, and nearly all other commercial ventures.

Earth would know then that she had to strike to protect her trade, and Mars would go along. Together, they could sway the Federation. It would be a simple case of either making a striking blow at Thule before she wakened all her people and got into full production, or being forever lost in the shuffle.

With such weapons, many of them quite simple in application, even though the science behind them was unusually complicated, Earth would have a chance to win, and to win as soon as she could turn out enough of the equipment. Earth was well equipped to run almost anything through her complicated factories in a hurry.

There was another angle on it that bothered him, too. He had begun to wonder whether Thule might not have wanted Jakes to steal the plans. It seemed too simple, unless they had deliberately let him walk out with them.

Jakes had pulled stuff from one drawer of a filing cabinet. But Thule must have inventions of military value that would fill a warehouse. These seemed invincible and terrible enough. But they might be rendered harmless against her. She'd had them for a long time, and probably had answers to combat them. She also probably had a great many more weapons about which nobody from the Federation would ever dream.

He hadn't even guessed that Federation scientists had actually made the proton cannon. That had been a carefully guarded military secret, and his father hadn't even told him. How many hitherto unused devices did Thule have?

He had a picture of Federation forces rushing out in full confidence because they were equipped with all the Thulian devices as well as their own, and then finding that none of them would work against Thule. He also had a picture of somebody on Thule who thought war was necessary using the theft of the "secret" weapons as a good excuse to move in before the Federation could build them.

Valin brought up the idea of the broadcasts again, but Bob realized that on this point Jakes was right, and turned it down. He expected pleading, but nothing more was said about it. If this was a major point in the Thulian strategy, they certainly kept their hands concealed well.

That bothered him, too. There was no sign that they ever noticed anything wrong. He couldn't make up his mind whether he should take them at their face value as polite, considerate and civilized human beings, or whether Jakes was right, and they were completely untrustworthy, masking all their hidden plans to ruin the Solar System by false action, meant only to convince him.

On one point both Jakes and Bob agreed wholeheartedly, and Juan was in violent disagreement. They accepted Valin's suggestion that they might like some music and had one of the little tape machines delivered, with a few hundred pieces of the most carefully selected music.

It came while they were out. They got back to hear something that was a cross between an anguished cat and a tin can being battered around by a stumble-footed mule. In between sections, for no reason, a female voice would come on in a high, nasal singsong.

If there was any rhythm to it, it couldn't be found, except for a few sections where there was obviously studied effort to make a pattern.

When they threw the door open and rushed in to shut

off the racket, Juan was lying there with a smile of sheer pleasure on his face, beating his hand up and down as crazily as the beat of the so-called music. He let out a squawk when they cut it off.

"Hey, I want to hear all of how it goes," he cried. "This is interesting music."

"This," Jakes stated flatly, "is what happens when a banshee goes crazy. Uh-uh. Not in any place I'm living. Even my Dad couldn't take that, and he has a tin ear."

"You probably don't like your music well separated," Juan stated. "You like it all mashed together like potatoes in a pot, all going all of the time, oomp-pah-pah, oomp-pah-pah."

"I don't know what I like," Jakes said. "This ain't it. Listen if you like, but not when we're around."

Juan looked up appealingly at Bob, but he shook his head firmly.

"The next time we hear this thing, Juan, it goes out in the hall."

Some people even liked Chinese music, Bob thought. Maybe Juan was one of them. A man's taste was his own business—but not when he tried to force others to share it.

They found out the next day that there were schools of music, even here. Emo brought down his own favorite tape. Juan fled the room in horror together with Jakes and Bob. Even Valin shook his head sadly as he went in to turn it off. It was a monotonous up and down screeching on a single string, punctuated by sudden loud rumbles that came irregularly enough to be shocking whenever they reached the ears. Emo informed them that it was pure ear-beat, but they didn't care what he called it.

But the incident added some variety to their life, and it was reaching the stage where they needed it. Thule was too well oiled and too smooth. Everything was available for the asking, which made nothing worth bothering with. They had seen the town, and had met all the people they cared to meet.

And again, they were simply bored with it all.

The trouble came to Jakes's attention first. "Aren't there any female Thulians?" he asked.

Bob thought it over. He hadn't seen one since they arrived, though there were enough pictures about to show that Thulian girls must have existed once—and rather pretty ones, at that.

Valin answered the question when they put it to him, with the statement they would have expected to hear. "No, the women have not been awakened. When there is war, why bother them. War is for men."

Bob remembered his mother, who had served eight years as a nurse on one of the ships before she met his father. And he remembered all the other women who were working in the shops on Outpost.

"I thought in a culture as well developed as yours, you'd have complete equality between men and women."

Valin was horrified. "We're not barbarians, Bob. We don't expect our women to fight the way the savages used to. Do you mean to say the Federation has females in its forces?"

"It certainly has. And volunteers too! What would you do if a woman wanted to join your military group?"

"It has happened," Valin answered slowly. "But we usually cured their minds."

Things like that would be no help in bringing peace about, Bob knew. Each side would continue to regard the other as technically well developed, but culturally savage. And neither would understand the other. He couldn't see how they got that way, himself, and he'd been trying hard.

He went back to his room to try to think of something to do that might be useful and interesting, and finally fell asleep. When he awoke, there was a buzzing that sounded like a mosquito. He sat up to look for it, before he remembered that there were no insects on Thule. They had been killed off thousands of years before.

But the buzzing persisted. He turned over, and noticed that the sound was coming from the table beside the bed. Then he realized that it must be his little radio.

When he picked it up, the buzzing became a frantic shouting of words—and in his father's voice!

"Bobbie," it was saying over and over. Then: "Bobby, here's daddikins. Keepum ear peeled. Eway ar-yay umingkay. . . ."

It went on in a mixture of Pig Latin, baby talk and slang. Translated, Bob gathered that his father had somehow gotten permission to take one ship alone and come looking for him. He'd managed with a newly im-proved radar to avoid the warning buoys sowed in space, and had come in close enough to study the ground. He'd even spotted the *Icarius* in Center Park, so he was pretty sure where they were. But he hadn't gotten much more on that first trip.

Now he was coming back.

"Get out by that long S-shaped park at the end of the city—the far end," his message went on in its crazy mixture of words. "There's an open spot there big enough for me to land. If you see me, come running, because I'll be blasting off at once. And if you've got any information, bring it with you."

The message repeated again and again, then cut off. Bob knew that it must have taken almost fantastic power to blast it all the way through space on that fre-quency and deliver so much volume on the little set. But it didn't puzzle him as much as the reasons for letting his father come for him. Wallingford must think he needed a lot more information on Thule than Bob had put into the simple letter to his father.

But it was no trick, he was sure. It had been his fa-ther's voice, and the silly jumble of words were just the ones which would carry meaning to him, but wouldn't make sense to a Thulian, even though English was un-derstood by some of them.

He looked at his watch, and hoped that it was some-where near right. The best time to land would be during the brief hour when Thule cut down the amount of light in the air to encourage the plants, which needed some rest apparently.

Even at best, there wasn't one chance in a thousand that the plan would succeed. But Bob had to try to take advantage of what chance there was.

CHAPTER 16 /

Vigil at Night

JAKES LISTENED TO THE PLAN, and shook his head. "It must be a fake, Bob. I don't care how convincing it was. Look, do you think Wallingford's dumb enough to send one man here when he's busy trying to build up a fleet for an all-out invasion. And with an improved radar screen!"

"I know Dad's voice!" Bob insisted.

"All right, so you know his voice. But do you know he is going to do what the message says? Do you even know that we're not the only captives on this planet?"

Juan sat up abruptly. "What? How did you learn this, Simon?"

"I got it out of Emo, of course. The kid will do anything I ask—he thinks I'm his own personal freak." Jakes lay back, watching the effect, and enjoying their faces. "All right, here's the dope—and don't go calling me a dumb spy from now on. Thule has a whole bunch of prisoners. They copped a whole freighter and a passenger ship. They've also picked up a couple of the men from Wing Nine who managed to live, and they put them back together. Maybe a hundred and fifty persons altogether!"

"Then why haven't we seen them?"

"I got a glimpse of them. Through a window. But they aren't running around loose like us. None of this high and mighty courtesy, and all for the love-of-studying-us stuff for them. They're locked up on the top floor of one of the buildings here. Emo says they get good treatment, and maybe he's right. But not like us."

He lifted himself up. "And if you want to know why we're being treated this way, all I can guess is that they figure we're young enough to make good suckers! Why else? Anyhow, if they've got prisoners—the ones from the freighter for months—why not your father?"

"They wouldn't know about the kind of slang he used," Bob tried to defend himself.

"They'd know we had some kind. Every language has slang," Simon said.

Juan nodded. "That is true. And it is very difficult to make a slang sound real that is not. If they wanted your father to speak to you in slang, then he would be made to speak to you in slang. I think Simon is right. Better we should not go there. It is a trap."

"I'm going," Bob announced shortly. "If it is on the level, I'm not going to have him risking his life for nothing."

"Well, you've got a point there. Hey, I know. That's it!" Jakes got clear off the bed this time. "Look, they found those papers missing. Only I did a good job, and they couldn't trace them. But they figured one of us must have 'em. So they want you to bring them out, and they'll just pick you up and get them back. Slick. As good as if I'd thought of it myself."

That was the best guess Bob had heard. It could be true—in the event his father was a prisoner. But he still couldn't be sure, and the feeling that the Thulians knew all about the stolen papers still stuck in his head.

"I'm going," he repeated.

Jakes shrugged. "Okay, be a sucker. Go ahead. But not with the papers! I've got my own plans for them. I'm getting in thicker and thicker with Emo, and with everything else I've found, I should be leaving here any day. These ideas are my own, too—none of the stuff being planted on me, like your message. You'd better stick around until then, Bob."

Juan nodded. "Simon has good plans, Bob. We can

take off in the *Icarius* all together and with the papers."

"You can keep your blasted papers!" Bob told them as he went out. But he wasn't happy about it. He'd been counting on their being wild to take a chance with him, and it hurt to know that he would have to go it alone.

Here and there during the day, Bob picked up a complete set of dark gray clothing of the style worn here generally. It was the least visible stuff he could get. His mind was only partly on it, though. He was trying to remember the exact phrasing of the message. Some of it had sounded strange at the time. That business about "daddikins" was odd, considering that his own childhood name for his father had been a shortened mispronunciation of Commander—"kanner." Yet, if his father had been in a hurry . . .

Jakes had ruined his faith, without giving him a good argument. And the two of them might at least have offered to help him, instead of being so smug about their own plans to steal back the *Icarius*.

But he should have known that they really meant to help. When he got back, Juan stood in the hall, holding a finger over his lips. Bob went up, and the boy leaned forward. "We've figured out how to get you free of Valin. Leave that to us, will you not?"

The problem of Valin had been bothering Bob. He nodded quickly, and went into the room to find the tape recorder turned on, and Jakes looking through a few of the reels. He was just about to put one on the machine, and his eyelid drew down in a quick wink.

"You aren't going to start that thing, are you?" Bob asked indignantly.

"I dunno. I've been thinking over that stuff we heard. You know, it wasn't so bad, at that. Kind of interesting . . ."

The caterwauling began as he finished speaking. It was a particularly vile example of Thulian music. Juan came in at once, his face taut with admiration. Behind him, a door opened, and Valin and Emo looked out.

"Get it out! Stop that stuff!" Bob yelled. "Either cut it out, or I'll put a foot through that thing!"

Valin stepped in softly. "My favorite piece of music, Simon. I knew you'd learn to love it. There where the *yornel* breaks through like a wave on a cliff . . ."

"Lovely," Juan said, and Jakes nodded slowly.

"Then take it somewhere else to appreciate it," Bob ordered. "I've got a headache already."

Jakes looked up at Valin. "Hey, do you think we could listen to it in your room?"

"It would be completely enjoyable," the Thulian said instantly.

Emo brightened up. "A good old steam session, that's what we'll have. I've got some tapes with me that are really round!"

They went off quickly, and Bob waited until the door was closed and the sounds of the tape began to shriek out in the other suite. Good old Simon, he thought. Jakes was really making a sacrifice for him, spending a night listening to that stuff.

They were apparently well wound up when Bob sneaked down the hall and up the stairs to the subway. He'd avoided the lobby, where he might have been spotted. In the Thulian costume, he felt he looked fairly inconspicuous, though.

The subway rolled along, while the automatic map drew a picture for Bob, outlining his route in green, and showing where he had to transfer. He made good connections, and was at the proper end of the park long before he had expected.

Killing time was going to be hard. He sat on one of the padded benches, trying to watch the birds and make some kind of a plan, but the second hand of his watch seemed to be standing still. He fell to examining the park carefully for a hiding place, and decided on a tree at one side which had low, sweeping branches that should form a good spot.

Then the air began to darken softly, growing darker each minute. Bob waited until it was hard to see details, then got up and walked toward the tree. Beside it, he paused to look for anyone who might see him, then ducked under the branches and crouched down.

In five minutes, his legs were aching, and he had to stand up to rest them. He checked the little radio in his ear again, but it remained stubbornly silent. There was only the dopey mutter of birds and the rustling of wind through the leaves.

Then, straight ahead, a branch snapped. Bob peered forward through the branches. At first he could see nothing, but then a vague form came into view, walking across the grass right where his father must be planning to land. It moved ahead until it stood with its head silhouetted against the whiteness of one of the walks, turned its face up toward the sky, and seemed to be sniffing appreciatively of the air or admiring the stars!

The radium dial on Bob's watch marked the passing of more minutes, and the man out there stood relaxed, his head turning a bit now and then, but apparently intending to park there all night.

Bob reached for his knife, regretting that he hadn't brought the gas gun he'd taken from Valin. He was trying to convince himself that this was a military operation now, and that the man out there was an enemy— an enemy who stood in the way of success.

He got the knife open at last, and balanced it. He'd been trained at throwing one, and this fitted his hand nicely. The blade was sharp, and the man was a perfect target. Then Bob let out a soft sigh of disgust and closed the weapon, dropping it back in his pocket. Maybe he was being yellow—but all he could think of was that the man was a human being, almost like himself, and one of a group who had never treated him with anything but courtesy and respect. He couldn't do it.

Abruptly, there was no need. The man took a final deep breath and moved over to the sidewalk. He swung off down the park, making a faint whistling sound between his teeth, leaving the place to Bob.

Half of the hour of darkness was already gone. Bob

moved out a bit where he could explore the sky above, looking for a tiny streak of blue that would be a rocket exhaust, but there was nothing but a speckle of stars shining through streaks in the clouds. Of course, the rocket might be behind one of the clouds, out of his view.

But it was getting late now, and he had to face other unpleasant alternatives. It was more probable that his father had been caught in the warning system, and that one of the super-speed missiles had gone shooting up to intercept him, or that he had been spotted coming down and was even now being carted off toward their prison. To have gotten through the net once and away again was nearly unbelievable luck; a second time would be a minor miracle.

Thule must have picked up the radio signal, anyhow. And Bob had no idea of how clever they were at decoding. If the language machine worked both ways, and there was no reason he could see why it shouldn't, then they would have had time to strip the minds of their captives of all the information needed to interpret it.

Jakes's words kept coming back to him. When he looked at them honestly, he had to admit that the other's explanation of it as a simple trap was better than any other reasoning. And in that case, they had already captured Commander Griffith, and they must be waiting patiently, enjoying their joke on Bob.

But there were still ten minutes left of darkness, and it would be stupid to quit at this stage. With the heat and light in the air turned down, it had grown cold, and Bob's teeth began to chatter faintly as he strained to see up through the clouds. He should have worn something warmer, but he hadn't been out in Thule's brief night before.

There was the sound of quiet steps in the distance behind him, and he drew deeper into the shadows. Normally, the people of Thule preferred to stay indoors during the darkness, but tonight seemed to be jinxed.

As he listened, there were still more steps along the sidewalk to his right.

Suspicion was stronger in him now, but he tried to play the game out by pulling himself up to the bole of the tree. His fingers explored above him for a handhold he could use in climbing up it, but the branches were just too high here. He couldn't jump for it without attracting their attention.

It was growing lighter again, moving from night to dawn in a few minutes. He huddled against the tree, unable to see through the drooping branches, except for a few inches near the ground. He could make out feet moving on the sidewalk, and saw another pair cross the grass—probably the man whom he had heard behind him. The two met and stopped, and he could hear their soft voices, too low for the words to be clear.

They stood there for a minute or so, until the full light of day was restored, and the last faint hope that Bob's father might still land had vanished. He edged around silently, putting the trunk of the tree between himself and the feet, watching to make sure he didn't step on a twig that would give him away. The voices went on, revealing that they were still there.

Bob debated trying to sneak away, keeping the tree between them. He could also just saunter out casually, as if he had been coming across the grass and had simply passed under the tree. If they hadn't been watching too closely, this move might not catch their attention. Certainly he couldn't simply stand there all day. Valin must have missed him by now, and there was probably a hue and cry going up for him right at the moment.

Then his puzzle was settled from outside.

"Bob Griffith," a voice called out quietly. "Bob, you might as well come out from behind that tree."

It was Valin's voice. Bob grunted in angry self-disgust and futility and bent down to come out. Waiting for him on the sidewalk were Ondu and Valin, both carrying the little hand guns at their hips.

CHAPTER 17 /

Council of War

THE TWO THULIANS FELL in beside him quietly, one on each side. They didn't draw their weapons, but it was unnecessary; as they had told him the first day, there was no place on Thule to hide. The whole planet was his prison.

Valin chuckled softly. "That was a nice trick you boys worked up with the music," he said quietly. "I still don't see how you got your parts down so neatly."

"It grew out of the first hearing," Bob told him. "I guess it didn't work very well, since you managed to trail me."

"It worked well enough for a few minutes. You just couldn't know that we had a button on your jacket that broadcast where you were any time we put a tracer on it. Would you rather walk or ride?"

It was obviously all going to be very polite. Bob's lips curled angrily, and then he shrugged. Anger wouldn't get him anywhere now. "Depends on where we're going," he answered.

Ondu looked at Valin in surprise. "You know, we didn't tell him. Sorry, Bob. The president wants to see you, so we're heading for the administration laboratory, where we first took you."

"We might as well walk, then," Bob decided. He set off in what seemed the most direct route toward the eight-story building. "I don't suppose it would do me any good to ask questions of you two?"

Valin shook his head slightly. "I think the president would rather take care of that, Bob. And I also think you'll find it a pleasanter walk if we turn off down here."

"Definitely," Ondu seconded him.

"Orders?" Bob asked.

They shook their heads. "Merely a more pleasant walk," Ondu repeated.

Bob could have told them that no walk was going to be pleasant for a man under arrest. He preferred the shorter way, and kept on straight ahead, past alternate parks and business squares. It was the main entrance to the city, but there were only a few cars and pedestrians using it.

Ahead, there was the sound of some kind of work going on, almost completely foreign to this quiet capital city of Thule. Bob passed down another business block and found a larger park on his left. The noise was coming from there, and he followed it to its source with his eyes.

Workmen were digging holes in the ground and tamping down a solid foundation, obviously getting ready to move the Navy patrol ship that stood at one side onto a permanent location. The ship was a new model, suitable for one- or two-man control, and fast; it was about twice the size of the *Icarius*. Emblazoned on the side were the emblems of a Staff Courier and Junior Commander.

Bob had stopped abruptly to stare at it, and the two Thulians made no effort to hasten him onward. They had tried to keep him from going this way, but now that he was here they seemed content to let him stare at it.

He knew it had been the ship his father had come in. The rating and branch of service were both right. It fitted perfectly. But there was no way of telling how long ago it had been captured; it could have been a week before or within the hour. Bob studied it again, and saw that there were no signs of injury on it. Apparently the capture had been accomplished without any major battle.

But there was nothing more to be learned. Bob headed down the street toward the presidential offices, with the two Thulians beside him.

In the hall outside the offices of the president, there was a small mob of people numbering perhaps a hundred and fifty. All were from the Federation, and Bob realized that they were the prisoners whom he had never seen before. They seemed to be in good condition, though none looked too happy. Standing at both ends of the hall in which the moving belt had been stopped were groups of guards with guns in their hands.

Bob looked over their ranks quickly, trying to spot his father, but there was no sign of Griffith. Apparently these men and women had come from the freighter and the passenger ship Thule had taken over months before.

Then President Faskin came hurrying down the hall with no pomp or ceremony and no body of guards. He jostled through the crowd of Federation citizens. They scowled, but nobody made a move toward him, and he passed through the doors and out of sight. A minute later, the doors were thrown open, and the guards began herding the prisoners in.

Ondu and Valin held Bob back. "Not with them. He'll want to see you alone, Bob," Ondu told him.

The doors had been closed behind the prisoners. Whatever went on took very little time, however, and they soon came out again, and were guarded down the hall toward the escalators.

This time when the doors opened, Ondu and Valin indicated that Bob was to go in. He walked ahead of them, and down the center of the room until he stood facing the desk of President Faskin. The man looked up and smiled at him.

"Good morning, Robert. Sit down, sit down. We're not as formal as you people of the Federation." He was speaking in perfect English, and the smile deepened at Bob's start of surprise. "Naturally, I learned this as quickly as I could; the only way to understand a culture is to speak the language. We learned that in the days when we had fifty or more languages on Thule."

He swung slowly to face Valin. "Ready to report on what happened, Valin?"

"Yes, sir. I tuned our transmitter to his receiver, and sent the message until I was sure he'd heard it. Then nothing much happened until we went out. I knew he had decided to act on it when he obtained some of our clothing in a neutral shade. I managed to substitute a locator for one of the buttons. Later the boys tricked me into leaving Bob alone in his suite, and he went out. I waited fifteen minutes before I followed. By the time I reached him, it was getting dark. Ondu went and stood on the grass ahead of him, and Bob drew his knife. He held it for a moment and put it back."

It went on from there, a bare, factual account that showed Bob hadn't been out of their sight for a moment after he entered the park. They must have used infrared scanning to see in the dark, since they reported every movement correctly.

President Faskin nodded quietly. "A good job. Anything wrong with the account, Robert?"

"No. Nothing wrong," Bob answered bitterly. Whatever their purpose, they'd tricked him very neatly.

"Good. Then you admit drawing the knife?" He took Bob's nod for an answer. "Why?"

"Because I thought the man there was endangering my father and myself."

"I see." Faskin seemed neither pleased nor displeased. "Why didn't you use it?"

Bob shook his head. "I don't know. I suppose because I've been taught not to stab a man in the back."

"But he wasn't a man, Robert," Faskin insisted. "He was a native of Thule—resembling your race, but totally unrelated!"

"What's the difference?" Bob asked wearily.

The president nodded again. "Um-m-m, a good question, Robert. It's one I wish I knew the exact answer to.

Is there a difference in whether one is human or Thulian, and what is it? I can't answer *that* question. But maybe you have some others?"

"I'm curious about how you got that message from my father," Bob told him. "I know my father's voice, and that *was* his voice."

"Certainly. But he never said those words. We simply cut syllables out of recordings of his speech, pasted them up on a new tape as we wished, and then smoothed them over where we had to. It's an old technique. Isn't it, Commander?"

Bob swung about abruptly to see his father seated a few feet beyond him. "Dad!"

Griffith smiled weakly. "Hi, Bob. Yes, President Faskin, it's an old trick. We've used it, too." He stood up and moved his chair to a position nearer Bob, while Faskin busied himself with the records.

"We seem to be good at fool missions, Bob," he said, "but Wallingford was in on this. After Thule dropped your note and picture, he thought we might work a prisoner release and perhaps get a cooling-off period. So I volunteered. Only instead of flying over and dropping notes, I came down for a landing. And according to the law here, that makes me a spy. I . . ."

Faskin had swung back and now interrupted. "Commander, in the two days you've been here, we've kept our index machines busy working on precedents and collating results. But I frankly still don't know what to do with you. Ignorance of our law is no excuse, as in the case of your own law. And you had the example of our own messenger-observation ship. You claim you can't be a spy since you were in uniform and in a military ship. We believe you are because you came inside our lines on the false basis of being a lone messenger, and hence not suspected of trying to land. As usual, we're proud of our own spies and very hard on others. I don't see how we can help executing you, though I'd regret it. . . . Yes, Robert?"

Bob had stared unbelievingly through most of it. It

had taken time to realize that the danger to his father was real. But now he was on his feet, moving toward Faskin.

The president motioned him back. "Sit down. We can talk just as well in comfort. You have an idea?"

"No," Bob stated, trying to sound surer than he felt. "A protest. Since when did a man's attempt to communicate with a son, from whom he had received no word, turn into spying on Thule? Are the ties of family here being ruined by war?"

Faskin shook his head. "Robert, you know that isn't so. We made every effort to send your communication to your father, and he received it. When relatives are known and communication possible, we respect it."

"Did my father hear from Simon or Juan?" Bob asked quickly. "They were living within Dad's home."

Bob hadn't been sure that Thule would regard the family important for enemies, but luck had been with him. In this society, nothing was as important as family ties.

Faskin nodded slowly, while Bob's father stared from one to the other blankly. At the president's question, he agreed that the two other boys had been living with him, but it was all nonsense to him, obviously.

The president reached out for a group of papers and stamped them. "Very clever, Robert," he commented then, as he looked up. "You learn our ways almost too quickly. Commander Griffith, I find your landing justified as parental anxiety, and dismiss the charge of spying. But I'll have to hold you as a prisoner, since you have seen too much of us to be returned."

"Thank you." Griffith accepted his reprieve with almost no signs of emotion. He reached for his pipe and seemed to dismiss that matter. "I gather there's not much chance of getting the other prisoners returned?"

"None, I'm afraid," Faskin admitted. "I've examined them and found them all in good physical condition. Your worry that they might suffer deficiencies from the diet here are unfounded. And while none of them know much, together they might supply bits of information that would be valuable military knowledge. We'll have to hold them."

"What about the charges against me?" Bob asked. He wanted to get it over with, but it seemed that important things were being completely overlooked.

Faskin smiled. "No charges, Robert. We provoked you into an attempt to escape in order to study your attitudes toward us under an emergency."

He turned toward Griffith. "Commander, you're the first man of the Federation with any authority whom I've seen. And you don't want war. I tell you that I hate the very thought of war. Yet here we are, enemies, getting ready to start the greatest war either of us has seen. What are we going to do about it?"

"Fight, I'm afraid," Bob's father said bitterly. "At least, everything we've tried to bring peace has made war that much closer. And this isn't going to help much."

"Meaning what?"

"Meaning your holding me." Griffith paused to think, then shook his head. "I'm not important, of course. But I've come to be considered the leading voice for peace. Now I take off to hold truce talks—and I'm either killed or captured. It will make peace seem completely impossible to the Federation."

"And we send a messenger ship alone over your Outpost, and it's fired on." Faskin nodded slowly. "That makes you look like a race determined to have war. All misunderstandings, of course. But can I be sure? Or are you sure? Commander, if I freed all prisoners and you, would it prevent this war?"

"Probably not."

"Besides now we'd have to hold the three boys. Simon Jakes, for example, managed to obtain some of our secret documents with plans for weapons." Bob grunted as Faskin confirmed his suspicions, but the president didn't seem to notice. "We've substituted false papers since then—but if he has a good memory, he already knows too much. He may no longer need the documents."

There was no answer that any of them could see. It was the most peculiar war that Bob could imagine. Nobody wanted it. But fear was driving them on. The Thulians couldn't risk having their secrets stolen. For one thing, the Federation was far ahead of them in methods of production and in manpower. Given a few years of peace, Thule might find itself actually inferior in strength, instead of ahead of the Federation.

And the Federation already had reasons to feel that Thule could not be trusted. From their view, Thule had started the war. The business of trying to take a place around their sun was itself almost an act of war to most people. If Thule made any normal gestures of peace now they would only be taken as tricks to gain time while they revived the rest of their people.

Yet Bob was sure now that Thule was more like Earth than its mere outward appearance. There was less difference between the race of Thule and the original inhabitants of Earth than there had been between various Earth cultures in times past.

Perhaps, at the first meeting of the two, things could have been settled. But then there had been no way to reach a full understanding, and mistakes had been inevitable. Now those mistakes had grown and multiplied.

For the first time, he saw no chance of peace, no matter what was done.

A sudden shout out in the corridor interrupted their dark thoughts. The guards threw the door open and looked out. Now the shouts increased.

Juan Román came running into the room. His face was stretched tight with the strain of running, and he was gasping for breath, crying hoarsely. The clothes had been partly torn off him.

He stopped beside Bob, and his mouth worked as he tried to force coherent words out. "Simon—escaping. He . . ."

He couldn't finish it.

CHAPTER 18 /

Hostage from Thule

JUAN DROPPED ONTO A CHAIR, and someone from the back of the room came up with a glass of some dark fluid. The boy gulped it down. He took one deep breath, and nodded.

"Simon's escaping in his ship," he gasped. "I tried to stop him. He knocked me out. He . . ."

Faskin shook his head. "He'll be stopped! He can't get the ship free, and if he does, he can't get away from Thule. The fool!"

"No!" Juan stood up now, facing the president. "No! He's kidnaped Emo. Using him for a hostage!"

The room was suddenly bedlam. There was a stunned silence that lasted less than a second, then a wild shouting as the Thulians milled toward Juan. Faskin had turned as nearly white as his orange skin would permit. But he was the first to recover and start trying to get order, banging a wand against a coiled copper strip.

Bob had gasped with the others. "It means war at once," he shouted to his father. "They'd forgive bombing the planet quicker."

Proof of this was already coming. In the days Bob had been on Thule, he had never heard an outright expression of hatred toward the Federation, and he had believed that the Thulians had gotten over all personal violence. But now they were shouting like a pack of savages, a few crying for death to all men from the Federation.

The guards were better trained, though. They were moving in to protect the three in front of the president.

Bob suddenly touched Juan on the shoulder, and turned. He leaped toward the bank of machinery on the wall and began running along it. Some of the crowd that had begun to come in from other offices must have been confused by his Thulian clothes, for they drew back.

He was almost to the door when the loud-speaker on the ceiling broke into sound, in the voice of the president. "Stop! Robert Griffith, stop! Men, stop him!"

But the sound had confused them for just long enough. Bob found the door and was through it, bowling over two people who were just dashing up. He sped down the hall, and was surprised to find Juan behind him. A quick glance back showed guards pouring out of the big doors, with drawn guns.

There was no time to take the escalator. Bob blessed the Thulian who had installed a brass handrail beside it, and was on that and sliding downward before the guns went off. He landed hard, with Juan coming down against his back. That knocked the breath out of him but he had already grasped the next rail.

Thulian clothes were a nuisance. They offered no protection to his legs. But he hardly felt the burn as he slid down the third rail. He was getting the knack of it now, and blessing the times he had slid down the banister when he was a kid.

Bob threw out an arm to catch Juan at the bottom of the last railing, and then pulled the younger boy around a corner. "Have we got a chance to stop Jakes?" he asked.

Juan blinked and shook his head. Then he nodded quickly. "You want . . . Yes, maybe. We *must* stop him!"

Bob nodded, and leaped forward as he heard the pursuing guards coming down the escalator, adding their own speed to that of the machine. He glanced at the street and saw a man opening the door of one of the cars parked there. With a single bound, he was across the sidewalk and throwing the man out of his way. Surprise worked in his favor. The man stumbled and fell. Then Bob was inside at the driver's seat, Juan yanking the door shut.

He'd seen how the cars worked, though he had never driven one. The power seemed to be electric, needing no starter. He pulled the steering bar back, twisting it a little. The car leaped to life and tore away from the sidewalk. It almost ran into the opposite one, but Bob yanked it back. For two blocks, he weaved about while the car gained speed; but it was enough like driving a car on Mars so as not to cause too much trouble. He got the hang of it almost at once, and settled down to making speed.

Juan reached forward and found a button. A high whistle came from the car. "Maybe this will clear the way for us," he choked out. He was having his second reaction from the physical exertion, but was getting control of himself.

Bob nodded. The whistle did help. But it also told him that the sound he had heard before was pursuit by the guards, and from the extra volume of their whistles, they probably had bigger and faster cars.

In a way, he had an advantage. Thule wasn't geared to violence, and would be more confused than in a Federation world, where crime was still fairly common. But it also meant that he probably couldn't count on the Thulians finding and stopping Jakes in time.

Fortunately, he knew the way to Center Park. He cut into a narrower street suddenly, having seen that it was clear. He swung around a corner, realizing that there were advantages to three-wheeled cars. This handled much more quickly than the ones he had known.

"Thank God you found me," he told Juan. "I thought you were all on Simon's side."

Juan shook his head. "No. Not for this. I thought *you* might be on his side and try to help him. It was to the president I was reporting."

It was a good thing that Juan had seen the risk such a

trick would bring, Bob thought. Otherwise, Jakes might have gotten away with it—if he hadn't already done so. While the situation had seemed hopeless before, nothing could be worse than the results of injury to young Emo.

"What will you do, Bob?" Juan asked.

It was a question that Bob had been about to ask himself, and he realized he had no answer for it. He hadn't had time to think. He'd acted on pure instinct, get there first, and depend on what he found for his actions. It still seemed the only thing to do.

The sudden spat of something against the top of the car warned him that the guards meant business. They had cut off their whistle and almost caught him. He jerked the car into another side street, almost running down two pedestrians. He'd have cracked up long before if there had been any real traffic on Thule. Then he began zigzagging toward Center Park, trying to keep out of the line of fire from the pursuing guards.

Then another thought occurred to him. "Those tractor beams that hold down the *Icarius*—maybe he can't work them! The Thulians found the papers and substituted false ones for them!"

"I know of that," Juan answered. "No, it won't stop him. He found that the papers had been changed. That is why he decided he must escape now, instead of when he had planned."

Bob was counting on the fact that Jakes would have gone as quietly as he could toward the park. With Emo taken along by force, he would probably have had to move along by stealth, picking subways with no one in them, and lurking at the furthest ends of platforms. It should have taken him quite a while to reach the park that way.

Something spattered against the car again, just missing Bob's head. Then the car bucked, and began to twist sideways. One of the bullets—real bullets, not wax ones—must have punctured a tire.

He fought it to the curb, and had the door open as it stopped. There were several people standing there, and he'd picked the place because of that. He leaped out, with Juan behind him, and dashed through the group. They would keep the guards from firing—perhaps long enough.

The trick seemed to work, and they still had a chance. The park was only one block away, now. But Bob couldn't head there directly. He swung around a corner, then dashed across the street. The guards would expect him to take the shortest way, which was straight ahead. Therefore, the only thing to do was to go around the opposite block.

His legs began to ache, and Juan was having trouble keeping up with him. He slowed down, recognizing his mistake too late. He should have stopped running at once.

Juan caught his arm, and pulled him into the lobby of a building. "Underground, then up," he gasped.

It would be better than going around the block. This time, they tried to look casual as they moved down the escalator. With their rate of breathing, it wouldn't have passed close inspection, but there seemed to be no one around to look.

A couple of men were standing on the next lower level, but they didn't seem to notice anything unusual as Bob and Juan passed them. Then ahead there was the "Up" escalator. They rode up it, keeping their eyes peeled for a sign of trouble in the lobby they were entering. It seemed quiet, and the street beyond was free of guards.

This time, as they turned the corner, they were facing directly toward the park. Ahead, through the shrubbery, Bob could see the needle nose of the little *Icarius*. It was still not too late!

They glanced about, then crossed the street quickly, and were behind trees that would conceal them from any passing guard cars. By sticking to the smaller paths, they remained fairly inconspicuous.

But now guards were beginning to arrive. Through the thin shrubbery, Bob could see their cars drive up, and men pile out of them. He viewed them with both alarm and hope. They might be able to stop Jakes's crazy plan.

The shrubbery thinned out for a space, and Bob and Juan had to find a way around. He remembered that there had been another of the trees with low-hanging branches to the north of the little ship, and began threading in that direction, trying to see what was going on at the ship. But there was nothing to see that made sense.

Approximately fifty guards stood at the far side of the ship, with drawn guns. They were watching something eagerly, but Bob couldn't see what.

The tree lay ahead then, and he slipped under it, and moved forward to draw back the branches for a view of the clearing.

Simon Jakes was already there, a wide grin on his face. In one hand, he held a long piece of string stretched out tightly and running back into the *Icarius*. With the other, he was busy taking a cover off one of the little tractor-beam installations that were holding the *Icarius* locked to the concrete base on which it sat. The cover came off, and he probed about expertly inside.

For a moment, his face tensed, as if something had to be done very carefully. Then he relaxed again, and tossed the tractor-beam gadget back easily.

"The right combination or it explodes—and just the right spots," Juan breathed in Bob's ear. "He explained it to me once when I was to escape with him. It locks itself, one place to the ship, one place deep in the earth, until it is released. But what is he doing with the string?"

Bob could guess, but there was no need for it. Simon stood up and faced toward the crowd of guards.

"All right, you," he called out. "Get over there fifty feet to the left. And you'd better make sure you keep any new arrivals from getting ideas. Hey, new arrivals!"

He was in his glory, the obvious hero, in complete

control of the crowd against him, and on his way to perform what he thought were great deeds. The amazing fact was that somehow he now did manage to seem like a dominating, forceful man, in spite of his appearance.

Waiting until he was sure of enough attention, he pointed to the string. "You see this, all of you. Well, if you don't already know it, this is all that's keeping a switch inside that ship from closing. And when that switch closes, your president's son is going to get five thousand volts right out of the engines through him. He's in there. Don't worry about that. He's all tied up, but he's perfectly safe—just as long as I keep this line good and tight."

They obviously believed him, or were afraid to take any chances that he might be right. And they had already decided that Emo couldn't be hurt without letting go of the string.

The crowd had already moved toward the new spot Jakes had selected. Some of the guards were moving about at the far edge, talking to others who were just arriving. And Bob saw more of them keeping a careful eye on all approaching cars, to make sure that no guard acted before he found the facts.

Jakes moved over to another of the tractor-beam devices, and waited until the watching guards were quiet. Then he began working on the mechanism.

Juan clutched Bob's arm. "What can we do? You know him better than I do."

Bob shook his head. He'd known Simon as well as anyone had known him. But the boy was never easy to understand. And Bob had no idea whether Jakes would trust him now or not. He'd been suspicious enough not to tell everything about his plans. And his experience with Juan, on whom he'd counted, had probably made him more suspicious.

Bob was still waiting for a break, hoping he'd have enough sense to recognize it when it came.

This time, Simon stopped in the middle of the operation to rest. Whatever he did to the gadgets must have required a cool nerve.

"How would he know what combinations these were set for?" Bob asked Juan.

"Thule made them all the same, I guess," Juan answered. "Or so Simon guessed. He thought that the explosion was from a sudden, uncontrolled release of the energy of the beam—that it was not intended to keep people from releasing the locks or examining the machine. They were not meant for war, really."

Now Simon bent over and probed again. His face broke into a grin of satisfaction, and he picked up the device.

"All right," he called out. "Now all of you keep back—well back. I'm going home."

Winding the string up carefully as he went, he moved toward the lock of the *Icarius*. There, he opened the outer seal, placed the tractor-beam device inside.

It had to be now or never, Bob decided. He broke out from under the tree and leaped toward the little ship. "Simon, wait!"

But either Jakes hadn't heard him, or wasn't interested. The little lock began closing before Bob was halfway there, and it snapped shut with a definite click, just as he reached it.

The guards who had been at the presidential chambers obviously considered it better to get in some action, and they also recognized Bob as someone they were to stop. With Simon inside the ship, it was time for them to do something.

The first bullet missed by several feet, but the second one was closer.

CHAPTER 19 /

Flight to Nowhere

BOB HIT THE LITTLE LOCK BUTTON with his fist, hoping that Jakes hadn't yet had time to seal it from inside. Then, just as Juan pounded up behind, it snapped open.

He leaped inside, with Juan at his heels, amazed at the poor marksmanship of the guards, which he didn't want to test further, though, for bullets were still flying. His finger found the button that controlled the locks from inside, and they snapped closed behind him.

"Bob!" Jakes's voice sounded happy. "Hey, doggone it, I was wishing you could have been here."

He was already settling into the control seat, but now he relaxed a trifle. "Neat, the way I fooled those Thulians! Had a piece of string tied to the seat, and they thought I had it fixed to kill Emo. You should . . ."

For the first time, he seemed to see Juan, and his face hardened. "What are you doing here?"

"He came to me, and I got him to come along," Bob said quickly.

Simon nodded uncertainly. "Well . . . we'll talk about that later. Grab seats, because here we go!"

He didn't wait, but hit the throttle at once. Bob felt the acceleration begin to build up, and staggered to one of the seats, while Juan found another. Then Jakes moved over to full high-drive, and they were lifting from Thule.

And behind them almost at once would come the ships from Thule. The war was on, as of this minute.

"What happened to Emo?" Bob managed to ask.

"Back of you, in the fourth seat. I had him tied in while I freed the *Icarius*. Hey Emo, how you doing?" Jakes's voice sounded completely confident now.

From in back of Bob, a high voice piped up. "I'm all right, but you'd better take me back, you had! When my father catches you, you're going to be sorry!"

"You'll like the Federation men, Emo," Simon told him. Then bitterness crept into his voice. "Did Juan tell you, Bob, that he tried to stop me? He actually started throwing his fists around, when he heard my plan. You'd think he'd sold out to the enemy!"

"He was right, Simon," Bob told him. "You had no business in starting this. I told you about Emo's position back there."

"Sure. That's why I took him. They can't touch us now, and they won't dare let us get in any trouble with that network of bombs and warnings they have."

Juan sighed softly. "Maybe you were right, Simon. But I was afraid. That is why I wanted to stop you until I could see Bob."

Simon cut the drive suddenly until the pressure on them was only a little more than the gravity of Earth. "Don't know why I'm in such a hurry," he told them. "We're safe enough with Emo aboard. Hey, you know, you're right, Juan. I guess I forgot about Bob. When I found those Thulians had switched papers on me, all I could think of was to get out of there fast. I guess maybe I was a bit too hasty. Okay, Juan, I'll forget it if you will."

"It is already forgotten," Juan said. "But what shall we now do with Emo? We cannot bring war about, Simon. And as Bob has said, to keep him from his family of Thule means war."

"We'll keep him, all right. Maybe they switched papers on me, but I can remember what the originals said. I sure proved that when I got the old *Icarius* free, didn't I? Anyhow, we always knew it had to be war. This just makes it come a little faster."

"There doesn't have to be war," Bob told him. "Right now my father is down there with the president, talking peace. Or he was, before you ran out with Emo."

It was partly true—talking peace and war. Bob felt suddenly sick as he wondered what was really happening now. If Thule decided to take it out on all the Federation people they had . . .

Some of the smugness went from Jakes then, but he stuck to his guns. "Aw, you can't trust Thule. Sure, they'll talk peace—and then, when they get us off guard, they'll take over. And we can't risk it."

"So you want war?" Juan accused.

"No, I don't want war! But I don't want to see our side wiped out because a bunch of fools thought talking about peace was the same as protecting yourself. Hey, look at that!"

In the screen, a flight of the great ships of Thule showed up. There were hundreds of them, and they were spread on all sides of the *Icarius,* matching her speed and waiting.

Juan stared at it dully. "They will find some way," he warned. "They have ways of freezing the air, of taking all the heat away at once. It would not kill Emo, but then they could catch us."

Jakes looked doubtful, and then shook his head. "They'd have done it already if they could. They can't do that through the walls of another ship."

"You hope they can't," Bob corrected him. "You don't think you know all the science of Thule, do you?"

"All right," Jakes suggested. "You bright guys have been raising enough objections to the one thing that's saving your skins. Now suppose you tell me what you'd do?"

Juan shrugged. "I'd put Emo outside in a space suit. Then the ships out there would stop to see whether he was still alive, and to return him to Thule. They might even let us go. But we would have time to get away, and even lose them."

He had moved up to the screen beside Jakes. "It would give them something to do instead of chasing after us," he finished.

Jakes snorted. "Yeah. That's a right fine idea, Juan. There are a thousand ships there, and you think every one would stop, just sit still, and then go back to Thule, if they had the kid. Nope! *One* would pick him up. And what was left of us would be dust—nothing but dust. Look out there!"

He stood up to see through the port better. Juan hit him with a hard shoulder, knocking him from the control seat, and was in his place at once.

Under his hands, the throttle leaped, throwing more acceleration pressure against them. Jakes slipped all the way to the floor, sprawling and moaning as the pressure hit him.

"I can raise it higher, Simon," Juan warned him. "I can raise it until you can no longer stand it. Or I can let you up to find a space suit for Emo and put him out."

"You'll get us killed," Simon gasped.

Juan nodded. "Perhaps. I do not think so, but perhaps you are right. It is still better than the war would be. Will you do as I say?"

"Let me up," Simon agreed reluctantly.

Some of the pressure slacked off, and the older boy crawled painfully to his feet. "Patriotism!" he grunted. "You think you're being a hero and a patriot. But you're not. You're just making us sitting ducks for Thule. And they'll kill us before the kid is through the lock."

He swayed as Juan applied more thrust. Then he nodded with difficulty, and turned toward the suit lockers as Juan let it up. For a second, he fumbled with the door of the locker.

Bob watched him, trying to think. He had no more use for Juan's solution than Jakes had, and he was sure that Simon was correct; as soon as they had the boy, some of the Thule ships would exterminate those who had tried to kidnap him. But it might help to stop this crazy war that was now already started. And he could think of nothing better at the moment.

Simon swung around suddenly, and there was a gun in his hand. "All right, sucker," he ordered Juan. "Get out of that seat! You've made enough trouble. I ought to put you off so you could go back to Thule where you belong! Get up!"

Juan's hands moved toward the controls, but stopped as Simon began putting pressure on the trigger. The older boy nodded. "Keep away from the controls. If you haven't got enough sense to search my pockets, how do you think you can outsmart me now—or outsmart Thule's ships? Up!"

Juan stood up—and leaped back at Simon. The gun went off, and the bullet ricocheted savagely around the little control room, just missing Bob's skull. Then Juan was on the other, and they were rolling over and over, each trying to wrest the gun from the other's clutches.

The *Icarius* went on, holding the same acceleration and course, since there was no one at the controls.

Bob got up wearily, and moved toward the two squirming bodies. He could hear each of them yelling for him to help, but he paid no attention to it. Then his hand darted down and came up with the gun. "All right," he told them. "You've done enough of that. Both of you get up."

He prodded them forward, until they were backed against the viewport and the radar screen, and then he slipped into the control seat.

Juan smiled, and started to come back, but Bob lifted the gun. "Both of you stay up there. Simon, I'm not going to stand by and see you get away with starting a war. I agree with Juan that we'd all better be wiped out if it will keep that from happening. And Juan, you know as well as I do that you can't save us by putting the kid out. You've got more sense than that. Anyhow, Emo wouldn't fit the suits, so they wouldn't recognize him at first. They might think it was one of us and take a shot at him."

"You can contact them by radio first," Juan objected.

Bob realized he wasn't thinking too clearly himself. There had been no time for real thought since Simon had first started the trouble.

"All right," he admitted. "You can. But I still think there are better ways. Emo, what do you think about it?"

Emo looked at him sullenly. "I want to go home. And you'd better take me home. You'd better do it fast, too, before my father gets you."

"Yeah. We heard that before," Bob admitted. But he couldn't blame the kid too much. It must be rough on him, and at least, he hadn't gone in for crying or hysterics. "All right, Emo. That's exactly what we're going to do. We're taking you home."

He heard a hoarse gasp from Jakes, but he was already beginning to swing the *Icarius* around slowly, to head back to Thule. Beside him, the great fleet of Thule swung in perfect formation. The move must have puzzled them, but they were willing to hang on until they either had Emo or there was no hope.

Juan started back to his seat again beside Bob. "It is a good plan," he agreed, and he was smiling. "You will have no more trouble from me. That is a promise."

"Fine," Bob told him. "Then take this gun, and keep it on Jakes—unless he wants to give in now."

Simon shook his head stubbornly and went on muttering about traitors.

"I suppose you think they'll kiss you on both cheeks and cry out about how wonderful you are," he said hotly. "Maybe you think you'll be the big heroes to Thule. All right, you guys. Have it your way. You'll maybe even be given a nice position there. But you'll hate your own faces when you have to live with yourselves. Look what happened to Benedict Arnold and all the rest of the traitors!"

Emo looked at him without understanding what had been said. The boy's face had grown more cheerful since they started to go back, and now he was picking up a certain amount of enthusiasm for the excitement.

"You're bad, Simon," he said. "You're a pirate, that's what you are. And I'm going to have my father make you sorry."

For the first time, the toughness left Simon's face. "You just don't understand, Emo," he protested. "Doggone it, I wasn't going to hurt you. Didn't I tell you I'd show you a real pirate when we reached the Federation?"

"A dirty pirate!" Emo amplified his former remark.

Oddly, Bob felt sorry for Jakes. Out of all that had happened, Simon had brought him more trouble than good, but he knew that the awkward, clown-faced boy had only been trying to do what he thought was best. It must have been hard on him to use Emo as a hostage, knowing the kid would dislike him for it, and still liking him.

"Sit down, Jakes," he ordered, more gently. "Emo'll get over it, I guess. And nobody's mad at you. So why start calling us traitors?"

Jakes came back slowly, his face uncertain. He sank into the seat behind Juan miserably, and Bob heard him muttering to Emo. But apparently the young boy was still angry.

Then Jakes's voice suddenly lifted to a shout. Bob grunted, but he was busy landing and had no time to look. If Simon started anything now . . .

"Bob, look!" Jakes was out of his seat now, holding Juan tightly in his arms, and the smaller boy was struggling frantically. "Look!"

Bob risked a quick glance sideways, and saw blood running from a cut on the back of Juan's neck, where he must have scratched it in the previous struggle.

The blood was a bright orange, unlike any human blood in the Solar Federation. And that could only mean that Juan was a native of Thule.

No wonder he had spotted the mock-up and had led them into a trap. No wonder everything they had done was known to the president of Thule. And even less wonder that he had been willing to let them all be killed to free Emo!

But it was too late to do anything about it. Bob had already landed and men were piling out of the big Thulian ships, heading for them.

CHAPTER 20 /

Peace Offering

THE SMALL ROOM off the president's conference chambers was air-conditioned and comfortable, but it seemed hot and stuffy to Bob. He glanced about, to Jakes who was sitting morosely glowering at Juan, and to the guards who had taken them from the *Icarius* and brought them here.

Almost no words had been spoken since they had landed, and he had led Emo out and given the boy to the crowd.

"So now what happens?" he wondered.

Jakes shrugged ponderously. "We get killed, I suppose. All I know is that I tried and failed. I still think I was right—and that thing sitting near you proves it, too. But right now, I'm busy praying you were right, and that something decent comes out of it. Why don't you ask our little friend?"

"I don't know any more than you do," Juan answered. "I don't even know why we're here. Besides, I was no more a spy than you, Simon, when you stole those secret papers. I just happened to be on the other side. Suppose I tell you, Bob. Would you like some of your questions answered?"

Bob had already guessed many of them, which Juan's explanation confirmed.

Thule had known that they would have to learn about the race they were meeting in a hurry, and had taken the first chance they found. They had captured a freighter, discovered all they could about the culture, and learned the language spoken in the Federation. A passenger ship later had given them more information. But they still needed more knowledge of military affairs.

Juan had been selected as looking more like an Earthman than anyone else, and a few minor operations had increased his similarity. He had gone with one of the ships then to locate a Federation military vessel and lay a trap for it. When they spotted the flight of Wing Nine, they'd hunted up the nearest freighter and stripped it of all its people and goods. After that, they had moved it to the right position, given it the right speed and course, and Juan had gone aboard, to play the part of the captain's son, since his errors would be less noticed if he seemed young. He'd sent out the first distress signal, as well as the second, and the whole battle had been faked. But Thule hadn't known which weapons were real and which were rumored, and their act of being a pirate ship had gone much worse than they expected.

In all other ways, their plan had gone very well. Juan had found a perfect spot for a spy, until he had learned all he could. Then he'd contacted Thule, and arranged for the trap in which the other two were caught. Bob, as the son of a Commander, was a particularly valuable person for their tests.

One of the guards interrupted his account. He nodded, got up and went out.

"Traitor!" Jakes muttered.

Bob grunted. "He isn't, Simon. In his eyes, he's a patriot. And you can hate him if you like, but I think he's a pretty decent guy."

Simon twisted about uncomfortably, and his face turned red.

"Well—well, doggone it, I never said he wasn't all right. Only when I think how I treated him just like a human being . . . Oh, all right." He stared at the door, and then slowly looked back to Bob, his face puzzled. "Aw, Bob, I guess I liked the little guy, too. And I liked Emo. Maybe I liked all the Thulians. But I had to put the Federation first, didn't I?"

"And I had to put the Federation *and* Thule first, Si," Bob told him.

The guard came up to them and motioned them to follow him. Jakes got up wearily. "Well, here we go. I wonder how I'll look in front of a firing squad?"

The presidential chambers were filled with busy men, but a path was cleared for the two boys, and they were led down toward the big desk, which, for the first time was not being used. The desk sat on the platform, but the chair behind it was empty.

The guard led them to a little door off to the side, and opened it, motioning them ahead. "Simon Jakes and Robert Griffith," he announced.

Then the president was in front of them, both hands outstretched to them. "Thank you—thank you for bringing Emo back to me. And bless you for bringing him back to Thule. In fact, Simon, thank you for kidnapping him, because without that there would have been no chance to bring him back."

Jakes's face mirrored all the things that Bob felt, but he was completely speechless for once. Bob stared in complete disbelief at the beaming face of President Faskin. "I don't get it," he managed finally. "You don't look as if you're joking."

"I'm not," Faskin told him. "I was never more serious. Robert, it was the one thing we needed. When Emo was stolen, it was bad—but when he was returned unharmed, and with no conditions, all of Thule was united again. They knew they could trust the men of the Federation, because those men were human—just as they were! You proved that you could give up something representing a long step toward victory for a chance to avoid war, and to do a kindly thing."

He made a sweeping motion with his arm, and the smile deepened. "It was the final touch to make them stop fearing the men of the Federation; and without fear, there can be no war."

Bob stared around the room, and saw his father busy at a small radio control panel. Juan was helping him. Griffith nodded.

"That's right, Bob. Within ten minutes after you returned, President Faskin was given the power to do what he'd wanted to do all along. I'd guess then the feeling here must have been hanging on pretty even balance between fear and hope, and it only took one good dramatic act to tip the scales. Oh-oh. Here's Wallingford now."

The radio had buzzed, and his father picked up a microphone quickly. It was obviously just a local extension of the big set located elsewhere in the city, if its signal was being beamed to Outpost.

"But what about the Federation?" Bob asked slowly. "It takes two sides to make peace."

Faskin smiled again. "I think you'll find in a war where there is no greed or hate, but only fear, that one side can manage to make peace, if it wants to. Even when the other side is already set to strike. We've just learned that your Outfleet is already near Thule and about to attack us. But listen."

He switched on a loud-speaker, and Bob heard his father's voice reading. ". . . all prisoners will be released at once, including some we didn't know about. You'll be given every secret of Thule's science you care for—repeat, every secret. Thule is prepared to offer every honorable factor needed to secure peace, and asks only the right to establish an orbit near Earth around the sun.

"In exactly one hour, you will see a force of one hundred Thulian ships approaching. Those are an outright gift to the Fleet, and the men and officers aboard are at your disposal. Each hour thereafter, one hundred more will reach you, until the Federation Fleet has exactly one-half of the Fleet of Thule. Since these ships are simple in operation, you will be able to train and install crews from the Federation within a few days, so need have no fear of a trap or treachery.

"And finally, the warning network around Thule has been removed, and the planet is now open to entry of any or all of the Solar Fleet. President Faskin has empowered me to inform you that Thule considers the Federation a civilized culture, incapable of conquering any world which itself is not bent on conquest. Thule is proud to welcome the Fleet and to co-operate in every way with the Federation of which she someday hopes to become a member."

He signed off, and turned to Faskin. "They don't believe you, of course, President Faskin. Who would? But they can't afford to pass up your offer. I think you can handle the rest of it."

He dropped a hand on the shoulders of Simon and Bob and started out of the little chamber. Then he turned back. "Juan, what about you? Feel in the mood for a real family dinner to celebrate all this?"

Juan's eyes searched those of the other two boys, and then he nodded quickly. "Even if you celebrate with the horrible music from Earth," he said.

For a second Simon stared at him, and then a grin of understanding broke over his face. He began explaining about the music on the tapes to Bob's father, while they worked their way out of the crowded, cheering chambers.

There was no fear on Thule now. There had never been hatred, Bob knew, because cultures sufficiently advanced do not have to hate other cultures through lack of understanding. But there had been fear. Thule had come into a Solar System where war had been common a mere two hundred years before, and she hadn't been sure whether men had outgrown it.

Bob and the others had done their share to prove that mankind had outgrown it. As the son of a military man, brought up in the tradition of a fighting Navy, his lack of warlike attitude had been important. But the real credit belonged to the little people who had hated war enough to make the Federation delay until the last possible minute, and then stop their invasion at the first sign that there was no need for it.

Men had proved that Thule had no reason to fear them. And now Thule was proving that it was safe for the Federation to accept her.

It was a week later when the three stood watching the last of the Fleet land for a much needed liberty, while other ships were taking off already to return to Outpost and to the other worlds of the Federation.

It was a busy place, this parklike landing field which had been his first glimpse of Thule. He watched the men of the Fleet coming out, grinning uncertainly as they caught their first glimpses of the people of Thule; but by now, they knew what to expect. Sailors hadn't changed much, Bob guessed. And the Thulian women who were now being revived along with the sleeping men were something to look at. Federation men and Thulian girls might never be able to marry, but they could still appreciate each other's looks and laugh together.

Bob turned back at last, with Jakes and Juan following him. "I guess we'll be going back to Mars next week," he said. "We'll have to get back for the fall opening of the Academy. 'Leftenant Griffith reporting for studies, sir!' That's going to be tough to live down for a while."

"At least you make it sound good," Simon Jakes grumbled. "When I say 'Leftenant Jakes reporting for studies,' I can't keep my voice from squeaking. I don't believe it myself, after all the fool things I've gotten mixed up in. Hey, imagine me going back to that old Academy to earn a commission when I've already got one."

Juan smiled at them. His face had been restored to its natural color, but he still looked more like an Earth boy than a young man of Thule. "You'll be back," he said. "With your father acting as first ambassador to Thule,

Bob, I'll be seeing you every summer. Maybe we can all take another trip next year in the *Icarius*."

"We'll take you on a guided tour of the whole Solar System," Simon promised him. "As soon as I get that inertia-free drive of yours installed."

Juan glanced up at the sky where the sun was already beginning to look bigger, and nodded. "It's a pretty good Solar System," he said.

Bob agreed. It was a fine Solar System, and it looked as if it would be an even better one in the years to come.

ABOUT THE AUTHOR

Lester del Rey was born in a small farming community of Minnesota in 1915. In 1931, he moved to Washington, D. C., to attend college, but dropped out after two years to work at a series of assorted jobs.

Reading and science were always his main interests, and he discovered the works of Burroughs, Wells, and Verne at an early age. After discovering his first science fiction magazine in 1929, he became a fan of that literature. His first story was written in 1937 on a bet to convince a friend that he could get a personal letter instead of a rejection slip from the editor of *Astounding Stories*. To his surprise, he got a check for the story, "The Faithful." Thereafter he continued to write off and on, becoming one of the most popular writers for the magazine. But it wasn't until 1950 that he turned to writing full-time.

His stories have appeared in numerous magazines and anthologies, and he has had over forty novels published, as well as fact books on atomic power, oceanography, photography, rockets, etc. He has also edited several science fiction and fantasy magazines, and is currently fantasy editor for Ballantine Books.

Among his books which he most enjoyed doing were some dozen novels for younger readers. The first of these, *Marooned on Mars*, won the Boys' Clubs of America award in 1953. Several others became Junior Literary Guild selections.

He now lives in New York City with a collection of typewriters which he rebuilds to his own requirements, a number of overflowing bookcases, and his wife, Judy-Lynn del Rey.